CLIFFTOPPERS
THE FROST CASTLE
ADVENTURE

FLEUR HITCHCOCK

For Auntie Frances and Uncle Max

First published in the UK in 2020 by Nosy Crow Ltd
The Crow's Nest, 14 Baden Place
Crosby Row, London SE1 1YW

Nosy Crow and associated logos are trademarks and/or registered
trademarks of Nosy Crow Ltd

ISBN: 978 1 78800 805 1

A CIP catalogue record for this book is available from the British Library.

Printed and bound in Great Britain by Clays Ltd, Elcograf S.p.A.
Typeset by Tiger Media

Papers used by Nosy Crow are made from wood grown in
sustainable forests.

MIX
Paper from
responsible sources
FSC® C018072

1 3 5 7 9 10 8 6 4 2

www.nosycrow.com

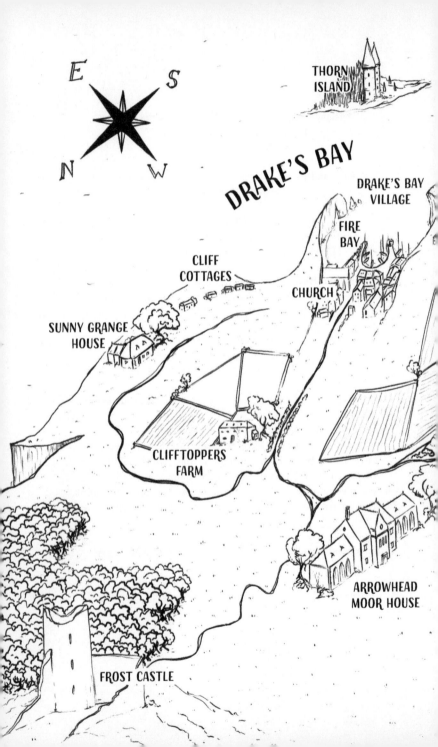

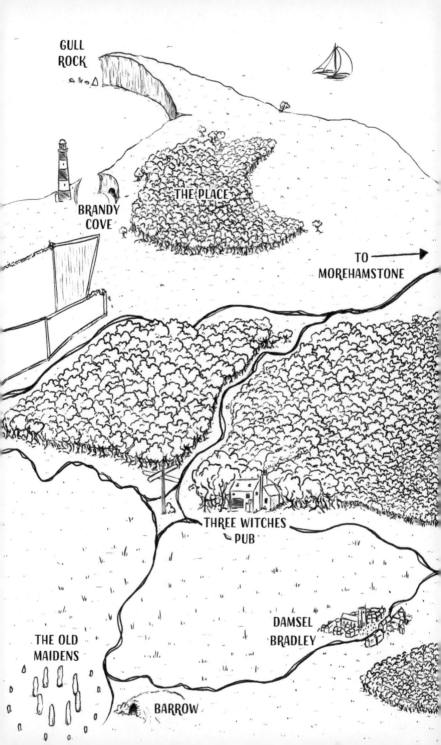

CHAPTER 1

It was snowing so hard, the path had almost disappeared. The only thing that proved its existence was the snow-laden trees on either side. Apart from the fact that his spectacles kept on fogging up, Aiden was extremely happy. He loved the snow, he loved racing around in the wild with his cousins, and he loved the fact that he and Ava had just defeated Chloe and Josh in their snowball fight at the bottom of the woods. They'd had to keep up a relentless barrage of snowballs to do it and the fight had lasted for at least half an hour. Right now, though, he was pretty sure Josh was sneaking around behind them and would mount an attack any second. For what felt like the millionth time, he took off his specs and defogged them.

"Whoop!" came a voice from his left and a snowball hit him on the cheek, sweeping his glasses from his hands.

"Josh! You total newt!" shouted Ava beside him. Aiden was vaguely aware of more snowballs flying through the trees as he fumbled on the ground for his specs.

"Argh!" shouted Josh.

"You deserved it!" yelled his sister.

Locating his glasses, Aiden wiped them off and looked over to where Josh was rolling around on the ground doing a full-on theatrical death, but still attempting to fire snowballs at them.

"Yay!" yelled Ava, charging towards her brother and dumping a load of snow on his writhing legs.

"I surrender, I surrender," shouted Josh. "It's all in my wellingtons!"

"Josh, you idiot!" yelled Chloe, running up through the trees. "We could have taken them!"

"No way," said Ava, cramming a last handful

down Josh's neck.

"Truce!" said Aiden, picking ice from his collar. "I want to go sledging – I need to warm up."

"Yes!" said Ava, kicking snow off a green plastic sledge that she'd been using as a shield. "See you at the top of the field."

Josh stood up, shook the snow from his coat and raced off through the trees to find his sledge, closely followed by Bella, their grandparents' dog. "Last one there's a soggy shrimp!" he shouted over his shoulder.

"No way," replied his sister, and Ava set off across the slope that led up to Frost Castle with Chloe at her side.

Following the two girls, Aiden waded out of a drift, dragging one of Grandpa Edward's homemade wooden sledges through the gateway and into the field. This sledge was heavier than the others. It would be brilliant at coming down the hill; it was just hard work to pull it up. He didn't mind, though. He didn't mind any of it – it was wonderful to be in the countryside with his cousins at New Year. And there was snow!

He stopped to bash clumps of ice from his gloves

and looked up the field towards Frost Castle. As he did so, he saw a yellow shape coming fast through the blizzard.

"What on Earth!" he shouted, pointing.

Halfway up the slope, Ava stopped, staring in horror as a small yellow car shot through a hedge, rolled once and slid on its side towards Chloe.

"Run!" yelled Aiden, too far away to do anything. "Run, Chloe – run!

"What?" shouted Chloe, looking back at him down the field. "What – why?"

Aiden gasped as the car continued to slide. "Run! Just run!" He dropped the sledge rope and half running, half falling, struggled over the snow, his feet tangling with Bella's, both of them barely upright.

Ahead of him, Ava sprang into action. She charged towards Chloe. "Chloe! Move!" she called. Aiden watched in amazement as Ava made a superhuman leap, tackling Chloe's legs and sweeping her sideways. The two girls somersaulted over the ground and into a snowdrift as the car slid past less than a metre from them.

"Wow!" shouted Josh, staring wide-eyed as the

car glided by him. It slowed, ploughed through a thick mound of snow and then finally stopped at the base of a small tree. The tree bent and snapped and dropped its load of snow over the windscreen.

The cousins stared at the car for a moment, stunned, before Josh ran to help Chloe and Ava extract themselves from the snow drift and Aiden headed towards the car. The doors and windows were all closed, and through the snow-covered windscreen Aiden saw no sign of anyone moving inside.

Ready to turn and run at any moment if the car started sliding again, Aiden put out his hand and pushed to see if the car had really stopped moving. It had.

"Hello," he said, stepping forward and peering through the windscreen. "Hello!" Inside, he could see a person bent forward, hanging from their seatbelt, their hands over their head. He tapped on the glass. "Hello – are you all right?"

The person inside uncurled, their fingers unclasped and, slowly, they raised their head. It was a young woman, and she was white as a sheet. She undid her seatbelt and slid sideways across the car, her head crammed against the driver's window. He saw her mouth something, and she reached above her head to try and open the door. "It won't open!" Her voice was muffled. "I can't get it to move."

"Hang on," said Aiden, leaning against the roof and stretching for the handle. It creaked and made weird pinging sounds but he couldn't actually make it open. He wasn't tall enough and the angle was awkward.

"Wait a sec." Ava appeared beside him. "Maybe if we both try. You pull, I'll try and get my hand in that gap and push from underneath."

Together with the woman in the car, they shoved and hauled and, eventually, the door inched open.

"Oh my goodness," said the woman, sticking her head and shoulders through the gap and reaching out to Aiden and Ava. "What just happened?"

"I don't know," said Ava as they helped her out. "Are you all right? That looked scary."

"Did I – did I hit her?" The woman slid to the ground. "There was a girl in front of the car."

"No," said Chloe, stumbling to the car, brushing snow off her jacket. "No, luckily, you missed me. Thanks to Ava."

"I'm so sorry," said the woman, half standing and then leaning back against the car. "It's just, so many odd things have happened to me since I started wearing this necklace." She clasped a small golden pendant hanging from her neck. "And this is the final straw. It sounds crazy but I feel cursed!"

CHAPTER 2

Scarves, middle of nowhere, snowing, yellow car sliding down hill. Cursed??? Why? Josh took a moment to write a quick description of the woman in his little red notebook. She was wearing woolly scarves, wound right up to her nose so he couldn't really see her properly, but he reckoned she wasn't actually that old. Maybe nineteen?

She was talking and he was half listening. "It's been a terrible few days. First there was my uncle's funeral, then yesterday I had to go to this crusty old solicitor and pick up the things Uncle Cecil had left me – which includes this." She pulled at the pendant. "And when I got back, I'd been burgled. So I had to sit up waiting for the police. I'm so tired. And now this." She pointed at the car lying on its side on the snow. Josh thought it looked surprisingly intact.

"A burglary?" asked Aiden.

"Well, attempted burglary – they didn't actually get in. My neighbour saw a man at the window of my flat, and called the police, so I had to wait for the police to come again this morning before I left, and then just after they'd gone, I realised that I had a flat tyre."

"Oh dear," said Chloe.

"So why did you decide to drive in a snowstorm?" asked Ava, holding her hands out on either side as the fat snowflakes landed on the palms of her gloves.

"I had to get to Frost Castle – I thought I was nearly there," said the woman, looking around.

"S'right there." Josh pointed through the blizzard to the top of the hill.

"Oh!" The woman turned to look up, and as she did so, one of her scarves dislodged, showing her full face.

Ava stepped back, her jaw falling open "Are – are you Martha Darcy-Court?" she asked, eyes wide. "*The* Martha Darcy-Court?"

"Who's Martha Darcy-Court?" whispered Josh to Aiden, who was rescuing a sled rope from Bella's teeth. Aiden shrugged. Josh wrote *Martha Darcy-Court? Who she?* in his book.

"Actress," whispered Chloe. "Famous actress. Starred in *Crystal Rose*, you know, the film?"

"That's me," said Martha, flashing a smile at Josh.

Josh turned his frown into a cheesy grin. *Celeb*, he wrote.

"Like, *really* famous," hissed Chloe.

"Yeah, I got that!" snapped Josh. He put his notebook back in his pocket and stared at Martha. She didn't look that special. *If she was really famous*, he thought, *she'd be driving a better car or come with a bodyguard or something*.

"So, what are you doing at the castle?" asked Ava. Josh could tell that she was trying to sound ordinary, not star-struck, but she was not succeeding. Her voice was all strangled and she had a totally stupid grin on her face.

"I'm in a play. It's a murder mystery, written by Felicity Meadows. She's an old friend of my mother's and I agreed to do it months ago, for charity."

"Oh, yes." Ava nodded. "They do something every year – pantomime usually."

"Well this year Felicity is trying to 'elevate' it. Get reviews and coverage, bigger audience." Martha rolled her eyes. "So, in a weak moment, I said I would take part – I think there are other actors too. Proper ones. It's just that the weather's much worse than it was at home and then, when I came over the hill, I lost control and you saw what happened…" She turned and smiled at them all. "Thank you for getting me out of my car – if you hadn't been here, I'd have been trapped."

"S'nothing," said Ava.

"You *were* lucky we were here," said Josh.

"But are you OK?" asked Chloe. "You haven't hurt yourself?"

"I'm fine, thank you," said Martha, shaking off a shiver.

"Course she's OK – look at her," grumbled Josh.

"She can walk and talk."

"Sorry about him." Ava flashed a smile at Martha, grabbed a handful of snow and jammed it down the back of Josh's waterproof.

Martha looked back at the car. "My laptop's in there, and my suitcase, and a rather pretty jewellery box that this necklace came in." She wrinkled her nose and blew away a snowflake. "Although actually, that could be in my suitcase. Do you think we could carry them up the hill?" She unlocked the boot and the bags slid out.

"Yes, let's get you to the castle," said Aiden, grabbing Martha's suitcase as Josh wiggled like crazy, shaking the snow out of his jacket. "It's freezing out here. We could take you the quickest way?"

"Good idea," echoed Ava, brushing the snow from her hood and taking the handle of the laptop bag. Josh glared at his sister. Going to Frost Castle sounded suspiciously indoorsy, not at all like playing in the snow. "But—"

No one was listening to him and Josh stared at their backs as they set off across the field. In an effort to slow them down, he took two handfuls of snow and lobbed them at his sister's back.

He felt a little less miserable when he saw that he had scored a direct hit.

As the snowballs thudded on her back, Ava tried not to react. She was, in fact, star-struck. Martha Darcy-Court was so famous. There was *Crystal Rose* and she'd been on *Saturday Night Singathon* and Ava simply couldn't think of anything to say that didn't sound stupid. Chloe and Aiden seemed able to talk to Martha and babbled away happily as they stomped up the field. From time to time, Ava would open her mouth and half form a word before feeling clumsy and giving up. She wanted to seem intelligent and elegant. After all, she was the oldest.

Another snowball hit her back.

"Josh!" she snapped. Why did he have to be such a total idiot?

"It's just here," said Aiden, holding the gate open for Martha. "If we can get through this path, we'll be at the side of the castle."

"Marvellous, thank you so much," said Martha, following.

Furious with herself and everyone else for being so annoying, Ava waited for Josh.

"I hate you," he said when he caught up with her.

"I hate you too," snarled Ava, tipping the snow from the top of the gatepost over her brother's head.

"Ow!" he howled. Ava gave up all attempts at being elegant and charged off past the others to avoid Josh's volley of snowballs.

CHAPTER 3

Stumbling through snowdrifts, Chloe ducked down beside a crumbling stone wall that enclosed the castle grounds. She looked up at two grim towers that loomed out of the blizzard. One of them was crumbly but the other looked complete. They were both unlit. An archway to her left gave on to a large courtyard and a shadowy manor house lay behind that. She couldn't really see it well enough in the snow, but she knew from previous visits that the house joined on to the towers.

Two small rectangles of light showed high

over the front door. Otherwise, the place looked deserted.

"Ooh," said Josh, stopping beside her. "That looks spooky."

"Haunted," said Ava.

"Seriously?" asked Martha.

"By the ghost of Anne, Lady of Frost Castle," said Aiden. "She only appears at New Year."

Beside Chloe, Josh let out a little squeak.

"What does she do when she appears?" asked Martha, shuddering.

"She howls," said Aiden, putting on a spooky voice. "And weeps, and she walks the secret corridors, rattling chains and calling for her long dead husband who was executed by Queen Elizabeth the First."

"How do you know?" asked Ava.

"Grandma told me," said Aiden. "She also told me that she opens doors and slams them again. It's really creepy. Felicity, the woman who lives there, doesn't seem to mind."

"Do we have to go in?" asked Josh. "I don't really want to meet a ghost!"

"It's just a story, Josh," said Ava, giggling. "It's

not like we haven't been before, every year in fact – and I've never seen a ghost."

"Anyway!" said Chloe, sounding brisker than she felt. "I think the door's round here." She set off through the courtyard towards the two lit windows. Before they reached the enormous door, it swung open and a woman in a brightly coloured cardigan called through the blizzard. "Come in, Martha, come in! I've been looking out for you, so glad to see you. And my goodness – Edward and Primrose's grandchildren too! What a stroke of luck! Have you come to join in?"

"Oh Felicity, I've had such a time," said Martha and then everyone began to talk at once, about the accident and the burglaries, about finding Martha and about how they rescued her from the car. But Felicity was unconcerned and wafted everyone into her hallway so she could close the door against the blizzard.

"How tiresome! Come on in," she said, kissing Martha on both cheeks. "Simply marvellous to have you, whatever the circumstances. And these little darlings – I could so use them just now! Coats off, darlings, coats off!" Felicity led them from the first hallway into a second.

The first had been large, but this one was huge with a roaring fire. Chloe shook the snow from her jacket, and looked in wonder at her surroundings. She'd been to the pantomimes before but had forgotten how amazing the house was at this time of year. The vast room was wood panelled and every gap and ledge had been decked with garlands of ivy and tinsel. The firelight danced from baubles that hung from the imposing wooden staircase, and an enormous Christmas tree bedecked with glass ornaments stood in the crook of the stairs. It was magical.

"So pretty," she murmured. "Like something out of a film."

"Wondrous," said Martha, from under her scarves.

"Does look good, doesn't it?" said Felicity. Her chunky jewellery reflected the lights and made her look rather like a Christmas tree herself. "I do love this time of year. I was worried you might not make it, Martha, dear. Now, I know you're Clifftopper children, but what are your names, eh?"

"Oh, I'm Ava, that's Josh, my brother, and these are my cousins, Chloe and Aiden," said Ava. "And that's Bella – our grandparents' dog."

"Of course I know Bella, we've met lots of times. How lovely to see you." Felicity held her hand out to Bella, and Chloe immediately decided that she liked her.

Behind Felicity, a door opened, and Chloe saw a look of wonder cross Ava's face. "Harry Hobhouse," Ava whispered, just loud enough for everyone to hear. Chloe watched as Harry turned his polished smile towards Ava. With a sigh, Ava melted.

Then Harry caught sight of Martha, and added massive megawatts of smiledom. The white teeth gleamed and his smile seemed to double in size.

"This is Harry," said Felicity. "My nephew. You may recognise him from *Strangers and Friends*, that television programme."

"*Friends and Strangers*," said Harry, walking forward, his hand outstretched. Ava reached forward and croaked something unintelligible, but Harry didn't notice her and headed straight for the swaddled Martha. He hugged her as if they were long-lost friends.

Josh stuck his fingers in his mouth and pretended to be sick.

"Shut up!" hissed Ava. Josh began to shudder with laughter, making it much worse by clamping his hands over his mouth so it just came out as a hiss followed by a high-pitched squeak. Furious, Ava kicked him, and he threw himself to the floor, hooting with laughter. Felicity, Martha and Harry stood and stared at him, which made it all the funnier. Chloe tried to think of something really serious, but felt the giggles bubbling up from her chest and watched as Aiden's shoulders began to shake.

"It's just, it's just," struggled Josh. "Her face..." He pointed at his sister and dissolved into giggles.

As uncontrollable waves of laughter began to sweep over all three of them, the door from the first hall swung open and the strangest-looking man entered.

"Absolutely hopeless! I've got a set-building crew, but no one to do lights and sound – and they're all far too ancient to be runners! Saw your car down there, Martha – shocking! Glad to see you look all right." The man stamped his feet. Huge lumps of snow fell from his clothes and his beard. "Good grief – a dog! What's a dog doing here, Felicity?"

"Oh Stanislav, do be quiet," said Felicity. She ran forward, plucked Stanislav's coat from his shoulders and threw it in the cloakroom with the others. "We've had the most stunning luck. Here's marvellous Martha, at last, *and*, rather handily, we have the children from Clifftopper Farm. They can do all that lights and sound stuff – isn't that wonderful?"

Bella took one look at Stanislav and growled.

Chloe shuffled forwards to trap her between her calves and surveyed the man. He was tall, bearded, and had a large nose. His coat was orange, his suit was orange, his shirt yellow, his tie red. He seemed to need more space than was necessary and he was definitely glowering. Glowering at Bella. In fact, glowering at the whole collection of people in the room. He even appeared to glower at the Christmas tree.

He took a long breath. He breathed in for longer than Chloe thought was possible, and then breathed out. But he didn't speak.

Instead, he swept his scarf from his shoulders, sending lumps of ice across the floor, and flounced from the room. "Lead on, Martha, Felicity. Follow, children. Follow, dog!"

CHAPTER 4

"This is so weird," said Ava, reaching up to the ancient phone screwed on to the wall. They'd been directed to Felicity's landline phone so that they could call their grandparents and explain the situation. "We can still say no. Everyone?"

Josh shrugged. "I suppose we could stay, as long as we can still sledge," he said, looking up at Aiden. If Aiden decided they shouldn't stay then that would be good enough for him.

He watched as Aiden considered the group of chattering adults. "I think we should stay, if we're helpful," said Aiden. "And I feel like something's going on here. What do you make of that beardy man – Stanislav Jones?"

"Apparently," said Chloe, "he's a famous theatre director – so what on Earth is he doing here in sleepy old Drake's Bay? That in itself is a mystery."

"Eating biscuits," said Josh. He pointed to the rest of the cast who, after hugging each other, and then hugging each other again, were settling around a huge fireplace in a collection of battered sofas and armchairs. They were making themselves comfortable with hot chocolate, freshly baked ginger biscuits, and little sticky waffle things. He rubbed his stomach. "Stanislav Jones is eating a LOT of biscuits."

"I definitely want to stay," said Chloe "I want to know more about Martha and her burglaries, and I'd love to find the ghostly passages, and we won't know any of it if we stay at Clifftoppers."

Aiden murmured agreement.

"I'm up for it," said Ava.

"Perhaps we'll find the ghost of Lady Anne?" giggled Chloe.

Josh felt less enthusiastic than the others. He

wasn't sure about being in a castle with a howling ghost *and* no one had offered him a biscuit. He sighed again – hoping his sister would hear it. But the others were too excited. He took out his notebook and began to draw the adults while he waited for Ava to actually make the phone call.

"Right – let's get going!" announced Felicity.

"Um – s'cuse me," said Martha. "I've left my script in the car? And some chocolates I bought for Felicity. Halfway down the hillside?"

"I can get them!" called Josh, stepping forwards. He could run down to the car, do a quick bit of sledging, and spend a joyous day in the snow!

But instead, Harry Hobhouse leapt to his feet and struck an unnecessary heroic pose. "I'll get it. Tell me where to go."

"What, right now?" said Stanislav. "Can't we just start?"

"Thank you, Josh. Go later, Harry," ordered Felicity. "For now, you can share your script with Martha."

Harry slid along the sofa so that he was sitting right next to Martha and glowed.

Josh drew a picture of Harry in the margin of his

notebook. Next to it he drew a picture of Martha. Over their heads he drew a heart and wrote the word *YUCK*.

"Oh, oh!" There was a sudden, loud cry. "I've lost my necklace! Oh no!" Martha had stood up and was spinning around, patting her chest and neck and staring at the floor. "But I had it earlier."

"It'll be here somewhere," said Felicity, examining Martha's cardigan.

"The chain must have broken!" said Martha as she shook her scarves out one after another. "It has to have done. There's no other explanation."

"What does it look like, dear?" asked Felicity.

"Just a – gold chain and a pendant thingy." Martha answered, distracted. "Sorry everyone – it's just rather precious to me…"

"We saw it," said Aiden, stepping forward. "You were wearing it after the car crash."

"Yes," said Chloe. "You said it was cursed."

"Cursed! How funny!" laughed Stanislav.

Aiden dropped to all fours and began to search the floor. He lifted the stupid skirt things that hung around the bottom of the armchair next to Martha in case it had been kicked underneath. It hadn't. For a moment, Josh fought the impulse to help Aiden search – after all, it was just a bit of jewellery – but he couldn't help it and seconds later he too was crawling around in the dust looking for the scrap of gold.

"Is it very valuable?" asked a woman who Josh knew as Mrs Edge. She lived next to the post office, had apricotty hair and was eating her way through all the biscuits. She wasn't helping at all.

"I don't know if it's valuable," said Martha. "It's just that my uncle left it to me rather particularly."

"I'm sure I could find it," said Harry Hobhouse, beaming for a quick selfie, then discarding his phone before rushing to Martha's side. "Now what am I looking for?"

On the other side of the room, a miserable grey man who Josh hadn't noticed before let out a long, exasperated sigh but didn't join the search.

Josh glared at him and then began an inch-by-inch survey of every scrap of the giant carpet, wondering how he had ended up doing this instead of whizzing through a field on a sledge.

CHAPTER 5

It took about ten minutes for Felicity to lose her cool. "OK, everyone!" she hooted over their heads while they all crawled around on the floor. "Please!" she shouted, clapping her hands like a reception teacher.

Noticing that the chaos was subsiding, Ava sat down and tried to look as grown up as possible. She crossed her legs at the ankle and put on what she hoped was a look of mild interest. She would have gone on looking for the necklace, but she could see that Martha had given up. Across the room, the actress sneezed and blew her nose sadly.

"It can't have gone anywhere. It must be here. But we simply can't lose any more time looking for it. We have only two days." Felicity surveyed them all. "Are we agreed?" She cleared her throat. "Welcome to Frost Castle – and thank you so much for coming through the snow – I know the journey has been, um, trying for some. And we've unfortunately lost a necklace." She glanced at Martha. "Anyway, we're lucky to have the wonderful children from Clifftopper Farm helping us. No matter what, we must perform this play. The community charities depend on the income, so we'll crack right on."

Ava watched Josh draw a very rude picture of Felicity and nudged him. He stuck his tongue out.

"Stanislav Jones is the distinguished director of our murder mystery. I'm hoping you've all learned your lines?" She snapped a smile at Harry Hobhouse, who was staring at his phone. "Right, so—"

"Who's going to be murdered?" interrupted Josh.

Stanislav Jones swung around and glared. Josh glared back.

"I will be playing Aunt Maud, and I will be murdered," said Felicity. "Quite early on. It means I can help do the backstage thingies after I'm dead." She looked around to see if there were any more questions. "In a minute we'll have a read-through. Ava – I've given you a few lines, darling."

"Me?" Ava felt a rush of excitement. Acting alongside Harry Hobhouse and Martha Darcy-Court was too exciting! She tried not to punch the air, but she did it in her head.

"The rest of you children, you're backstage, and I will show you where you'll be operating." Below the cast list was a scribbled list of backstage roles. Ava stared down at them, trying to look as laid-back as possible. Chloe and Aiden were doing lighting and sound together and Josh was the runner.

"What's a *runner*?" Josh whispered.

Ava flapped her hand at him. She was an actress now. She tried to concentrate on what Felicity was saying, but Josh hadn't stopped.

Turning to his left, he nudged Chloe and pointed at the description next to his name. She shrugged, pointed at the word *sound* next to her name and pulled a look of pure horror.

Josh mimed a slow death.

Ava could tell that Josh was building up to something worse, when she noticed everyone had gone quiet and was looking at him.

"How old are you, Josh?" said Felicity.

"Nine," said Josh. "And she's ten." He pointed at Chloe, who giggled and sat up in her chair. "And she's thirteen," he said pointedly, staring at Ava, who glared back. "Well, you are," he hissed.

"And you?" Stanislav Jones peered doubtfully at Aiden.

"Me?" said Aiden. "I'm twelve."

There was a silence and then, from the back of the room, the grey man spoke. "Are we relying on these children to perform alongside us? Are they our technical know-how?"

"Well, yes – they're the lovely children of my friends, Primrose and Edward. They rescued Martha from a nasty car accident, and I'm sure they're highly talented. Although you might not be able to see that right now," said Felicity, looking doubtfully at Josh.

Stanislav Jones let out the longest and saddest sigh yet. He leaned over, placed his forehead in his hands, and then raised his head and stared at the wall in front of him. "Oh, Felicity. I was so looking forward to this production, but now…" He rose from his chair, stretched his arms out on either side and said in a quiet voice, "We have so much work to do!"

CHAPTER 6

"How does this stupid thing work?" Chloe asked Bella, stroking the dog's ears while she stared at the sound console.

Ten minutes earlier, bringing her into the makeshift theatre set up in the Great Hall, Felicity had waved vaguely at a balcony halfway up the wall at the end of the huge room. "You'll find all the sound equipment in the Minstrels' Gallery. They used to play instruments up there while people danced. The stairs are at the side. I can't remember how the machine functions, but you're young, you'll work it out." Felicity had wafted out through the panelled doors back into the rehearsal room and Chloe had been left in the huge echoey space alone.

It had taken her five minutes to work out that the door to the gallery was disguised as a piece of wall, the only clue being the small brass door handle. Behind the door, a dusty staircase led to the balcony and to the unpromising machine in front of her. Thick dust coated everything and despite flicking every switch and pressing every button, she couldn't even get it to turn on.

Perhaps it wasn't actually plugged in?

Crouching knee-deep in dust and ancient sweet wrappers, Chloe reached underneath the table, her hand making contact with a dangling cable. "Ah, that makes sense," she said, grasping it and feeling along until she found the plug. Assuming that there was a socket on the wall behind, she placed her hand flat on the panel and fumbled around in search of it.

Clunk.

Chloe sat back. Did the wall just move?

Breathing out across the dusty floor, she lay on

her stomach and stretched her arms in front of her. The wall had moved! There was a thin strip of light all the way around the panel. A secret door?

Chloe squashed under the table and pushed the panel back until it swung open, revealing a long passage.

"What do you reckon, Bella?" she asked.

In answer, Bella trotted over Chloe's head and into the space.

Disappointed by his miserable role as a runner, which he'd discovered meant general dogsbody, Josh had gone to look for Chloe in the Minstrels' Gallery. But she wasn't there. Instead there was a tempting hole in the wall. He peered at it. Was this where Lady Anne would do her ghostly walks? But there was light coming from the other side, and it looked so interesting. He shouted, "Chloe?" After three shouts, each louder than the last, he stepped inside.

Much to his surprise, the hole didn't lead to a spidery stone-walled passage. Its walls were clean and painted yellow, and it was well-lit by daylight coming through a series of small square windows.

He looked back to see where he'd come from. The little door was quite obvious. He wouldn't have any difficulty finding a way back. And it was daytime. Ghosts didn't hang about in the daytime. Did they?

He wandered along the corridor until it turned a corner. Now he found himself in a long passage lined with picture frames. It would be about the right length for the Great Hall. He stopped and listened for Chloe but there was no sound except for the distant rattling of scaffolding poles. They sounded close, as if the wall was paper thin. It was the strangest feeling, walking along a narrow space that no one could see into. He stopped. No one could see in, but could he see out? Perhaps that's what the empty picture frames were. Running his hands around the side of one of the frames, he realised it was a flap. He swung it open.

Oh yes! This was brilliant. He could see right down into the Great Hall. He could see the scaffolding poles now and Aiden struggling with the lights. Excellent! Maybe that's what this tunnel was for – spying on people. He let the flap fall and walked on until he reached a T-junction. "Hmm," he said, peering down the two new passages which were not quite as brightly lit, and feeling ever so slightly creeped out. "Which way?"

Using the idea that turning left, left and left again would probably bring him back to where he began, he tried it, and soon ended up in a room that seemed to be part of the actual castle tower. "Cool," he said, enjoying the tiny slit windows that looked out into the blizzard. Opening a door on the far side, he found a spiral staircase. "Up or down?" he said to himself, and he decided on up. He raced up thirty steps, passing a landing on the way, and stopped at a battered wooden door. It was much colder up here, and when he opened it, he found himself in a freezing, dark space. Icy wind whistled through, howling and groaning and flapping some grubby plastic as it travelled.

Above his head a thin female voice called. "Jooooooosh! Are you there…"

Josh froze.

"Joooooosh… I'm coming to find you!"

Yikes!" yelped Josh, turning and racing back down the stairs, a thousand imaginary ghosts in pursuit.

CHAPTER 7

Chloe could hear Josh. He was here somewhere; she could hear him skidding down the corridors. No one else ran around like that.

"Josh!" she called, stopping at a junction and listening. Bella stood beside her, also listening.

She heard the skid above her head and ran for a spiral staircase at the end of the passage, but Bella was there first, vanishing up the steps, yapping.

"Josh! Are you there?"

Thumps sounded from overhead and Bella barked.

"Josh! I'm coming to find you!" yelled Chloe.

A long skid ended with a thump and a giggle and Josh stumbled away from the staircase and flopped on to the floor, where Bella immediately stood over him, licking his face.

"Why didn't you stop?" asked Chloe.

"I thought you were Lady Anne – get off, Bella!"

"For real?" laughed Chloe.

Josh scowled and changed the subject. "Have you looked through those?" he said, pointing up at the line of holes in the wall.

"Ooh, look, you can see the rehearsal room!" Chloe peered down, watching the actors bustling about. "Josh, do you reckon Martha's necklace could have been stolen?" she said, suddenly.

"A hundred per cent I do!" said Josh. "I mean – where is it otherwise? We looked everywhere for it. It's brilliant you think so too! I'm going to make notes on the suspects."

She heard Josh open his notebook and peeked over his shoulder. There were some very unflattering drawings of the cast. She watched as he wrote: *Stanislav Jones. Director. Bossy, but funny, though not on purpose. Horrible orange suit. Bearded. Angry. Doesn't like*

Bella. BIG BLACK MARK. Keeps on staring at Martha. He sucked the end of his pencil and then wrote. *Fish out of water. VERY fishy.*

"What do you think about Harry?" asked Chloe, looking back at the rehearsal room as Harry began to read his part. She was disappointed. He didn't seem either interested or talented and just kept taking selfies of himself and Martha all the time. She looked over at Josh's notebook. *Objectionable* he wrote, stabbing a hole in the paper with his pencil. And *Self-obsessed.*

"Ava's staring at Harry like a love-sick cabbage," he said in disgust.

"But do you think he could be a thief?"

"Too stupid," said Josh, drawing a huge mobile phone next to Harry. Next, he wrote, *Martha. Red nose, keeps sneezing. Car in hedge.* "Would she steal her own necklace?" he asked.

"No – nor Mrs Edge. Nor Felicity. I mean, she's a friend of Grandma's."

Chloe looked along the line to the grey man at the end. "There's Robin Baird. What about him? He doesn't look a bit like an actor. More like a bank manager or something."

Very dull, wrote Josh. And then he added an extra *very*. *Very very dull*. "None of them look like robbers," he said, studying the pages in his notebook.

"And no sign of Lady Anne, either," said Chloe, crouching down and giving Bella a hug. She was disappointed, she'd hoped for a ghost.

"Wrong time of day, I s'pect," said Josh, looking around slightly nervously.

Chloe stood up and headed towards what she hoped was the Minstrels' Gallery. "Come on, we can tell the others about this."

"Hang on a mo," said Josh, taking a last look through the peephole.

"Whhhooooooo!" A massive gust of wind bowled down the corridor, ruffling Bella's fur and making Chloe's hair stand on end.

"What was that?" she said.

A second gust howled along the passage, sucking the door to the Minstrels' Gallery open and then slamming it shut.

Bang!

"Yow!" Chloe yelped, breaking into a run.

But Josh was faster. "I'm out of here!" he shouted, whizzing past.

A little later, when the adult actors were "feeling their roles", Josh and Ava and Chloe settled by Felicity's giant fireplace to discuss the missing necklace.

"I think it's been stolen," said Ava.

"Chloe and I do, too," said Josh. "We've been watching the suspects from a secret place."

"What secret place?" asked Aiden, coming over to join them.

"Well," said Chloe, "when I was in the sound place I went through a hole at the back."

"It's like a hole in the wall – an actual hole," interrupted Josh.

Chloe glared. "It's a door. And – there are a load of passages that run all through the castle, they take you to the Great Hall, up to the old towers and past all kinds of rooms we haven't seen into."

"Wow! Do you think anyone knows about them?" asked Ava.

"I do," said Chloe. "It's all clean and tidy. And there are spy holes all the way along which let you see into the big rooms." Chloe looked up towards a painting high on the wall above them. "The hole into this room is up there somewhere."

"Creepy!" said Ava.

"And we definitely met the ghost!" said Josh, looking at Chloe. "Didn't we?"

"Maybe," said Chloe.

"But did you see anything useful?" said Ava.

Josh shook his head. "Not really," he admitted.

"Right," said Aiden. "Observe everything. Listen to everything. Search everything. Either that necklace has fallen down a wormhole into another galaxy, or someone's got it in their pocket. I'm sure we can find out who if—"

"Now, lovies," twittered Felicity, bursting into their circle with a tray piled high with biscuits and crisps. "I've brought you some supplies and a jug of hot chocolate – how does that sound?"

"Brilliant," said Aiden. "Absolutely brilliant."

CHAPTER 8

"So, I reckon, that before the end of the play, pasty love-face Harry will have married millionaire Martha. What d'you think?"

After their hot chocolate, Felicity had put Josh and Aiden to work, moving lights from the cloakroom into the Great Hall.

"I don't know, but can you just make sure no one's coming?" said Aiden, concentrating on working his way along the line of everyone's damp coats and scarves, rummaging in each pocket in turn. He felt horrible doing it, but they needed to check that the necklace wasn't there. He checked every inch of Martha's jacket, shaking out the sleeves and cuffs just in case the necklace was lodged there. He hung the jacket at the far end of the rack on its own, and turned back to search the next one in line.

"That's no good – what you need to do is this!" said Josh, grabbing the rest of the coats and throwing them on the ground, shaking them as if he was wrestling a pack of crocodiles.

"Josh! No!" yelped Aiden. "Someone might—"

Just at that moment Aiden heard footsteps on the stone steps outside.

"Whoops!" said Josh, grabbing the coats and trying to lift them back on to the hooks.

Aiden grabbed them and pushed them back against the wall, before leaning on them and trying to look casual.

"Hello!" said Stanislav, appearing through the doorway, bashing snow from his gloves. "What are you boys up to?"

"Um – moving the lights to the hall?" said Josh, pointing at the two huge egg-shaped lamps they'd removed from the cupboard.

"Are you?" said Stanislav. "Looks to me like

you're playing hide and seek in the coats!"

"Oh! Sorry," said Aiden, wishing he'd thought that one up himself. "We got bored."

"Fine, fine," said Stanislav, slipping his coat off and then rubbing his hand over Josh's curly hair. Aiden knew Josh hated it when people did that. He was impressed that Josh just let it happen without snapping. Instead, Josh put on a cheesy smile, and managed to look about five years old. "Just make sure you do get those lights into the hall. Someone called Jeffers is supposed to be hanging them up there this afternoon. With Jake – do you know Jake?"

"Of course!" Aiden said, beaming his beamiest smile.

They watched Stanislav climb the stairs and as soon as he was out of sight, Aiden grabbed the coat he was leaning on and hoisted it on to the hook above.

"Phew!" said Josh, sliding to the ground. "That was close. Oh! Hey! Look, Aiden."

Aiden stopped tidying the jackets and glanced down as Josh picked something up from the floor.

There, glittering in the middle of his palm, was

the necklace, pendant and all.

"Where was it?" gasped Aiden.

"Just here, but I don't know where it came from," said Josh, looking sadly into his hand. "It might have fallen from any of the coats. Anyone could have had it."

Aiden resisted the impulse to say something rude. Instead, he said, "Anyone except Martha."

"Corr-ect!" said Josh. "Anyone except the one person it belongs to."

Struggling with an armful of lamps each, the boys ran together into the hall.

"Chloe! Chloe! We're here!"

Josh dumped his light in the corner and stopped to look up at the Minstrels' Gallery.

"Do you think she's up there or crawling around in the corridors?"

"'Crawling around in the corridors'? That actually sounds quite interesting," said a voice from the back of the hall. Aiden looked up. It was Robin Baird, carrying a huge folded sheet of scenery. Aiden nudged Josh and quickly held his finger over his lips. Josh nodded.

"Oh, it is," said Josh. "Kind of."

"Got to be better than this shambles." Robin dumped the fabric on the stage. "You all right up there, Jake?"

Jake, a fisherman from the village, was clambering around on the scaffolding and the whole thing was shaking in a way that suggested it could collapse. They were going to hang the lights up there? Seriously? Was that safe?

"Yes – give us a hand, will you?" came the cry from the top of the ladder.

Robin climbed up the ladder and Aiden watched him clamber on to the scaffolding.

"I'll be mad if Chloe finds a way through at the top of the old castle. I couldn't work out how to get out," said Josh.

Still staring up at the two men on the scaffolding, Aiden asked, "So can you get out in other places or just in the gallery?"

"Oh – there are doors all over the place. There's even one right at the end here, I think." Josh led Aiden around the scaffolding tower to the back of the hall. "They're mostly invisible from the outside – really hidden." Josh walked along the wall sideways, holding his palms flat, feeling the panelling. "Here, look!" he said, beckoning Aiden. "See?" He gave the wall a shove and it swung open.

"Well, I never," said Robin, looking down at them from the top of the tower. "An invisible door. What a wonderful thing. Thank you for pointing it out!"

CHAPTER 9

At lunch, Josh and Aiden ran over, beaming, and practically sat on top of Chloe and Ava.

"What is it?" yelped Ava. "Get off, Josh!"

"Look," whispered Josh, and he dropped the necklace into Ava's hand, explaining where they'd found it.

"Oh wow!" breathed Chloe. "And look, the chain's done up. Or did you do that?"

"No, we didn't," said Josh. "It was like that when we found it."

"So, it can't have fallen off," said Aiden.

"We'd better give it back," said Ava.

"Let's just look at it first," said Chloe, peering at the pendant. "Have you had a good look, Aiden?"

"We didn't get a chance. Too many people around." He turned. "Oh, Martha! Look, we found your necklace."

"Goodness! How wonderful! Thank you!" Martha landed a kiss on each of the cousins' heads. "Where was it?" She took the necklace from Chloe's outstretched palm and sat on the end of the sofa, fiddling with the clasp.

"In the cloakroom – but," Aiden hesitated. "It definitely didn't fall out of your stuff." He glared at Josh. "Unfortunately, the other coats got in a muddle and so I don't know where it came from."

"Well, I don't mind, I'm thrilled. I expect it just got caught up on on somebody's clothes when we were all hugging hello."

Aiden and Josh exchanged glances. "Maybe…" said Aiden.

"I'm sure there was a rational explanation," said Martha. "I mean, you don't think anyone stole it, do you? No one here would do that, surely."

The cousins looked at each other in silence.

"Would they?" Martha asked, holding it up in front of her face. "I mean, it's tiny. There's not much gold in there and the chain's nothing special."

"Can I have a look at it?" asked Chloe.

"Of course." Martha handed Chloe the necklace. While they all chatted, Chloe examined the chain and the little pendant. It was an ordinary sort of a chain, not very thick or heavy, and it looked quite new. From it hung an oval-shaped pendant. It was about the same size as a foiled-wrapped chocolate mini-egg, only flatter, with some fiddly gold bobbles on the outside and a red stone. It was quite heavy, but not heavy enough to be solid. It looked very old.

"Does it open?" Chloe asked Martha.

"Open?" Martha looked puzzled. "Oh, no, I don't think so – it's just hollow, I suppose."

"Oh," said Chloe, peering hard at the thing lying in her hand. "Funny, it looks as if it ought to have something inside."

"Yes, I thought that," said Martha. "When Uncle Cecil left it to me, I was surprised. Pretty, but such an odd gift. It just came in the box with some broken bits of other things. Terrible thing to say but I thought I was his favourite, and then he left all the money to my cousins. Anyway, I can't work out how it opens even if it does. Oh – look, everyone's coming back in."

The actors were not as thrilled as Ava thought they ought to be when they heard about the necklace.

"I expect it was there all the time, in your coat. What a fuss over nothing," said Mrs Edge.

Robin Baird looked bored, and Harry Hobhouse slightly disappointed.

"Well, thank goodness!" said Felicity. "What a kerfuffle."

"Where did you find it?" asked Stanislav.

Aiden looked at Ava. She glared back. "It fell out of the coats," he said, "when we were playing hide and seek."

"Now that little mystery's solved, I could go and fetch your stuff from the car," volunteered Harry. "If it's a good time? I'm not in this scene."

"I'll go too," said Ava. "I'll show you where it is."

"Me too," said Josh.

"Josh – no!" said Ava. "You don't need to. We're just getting a box of chocolates and a script."

"I'm not missing my chance to go sledging," he whispered.

"Do I need kids with me?" said Harry, staring down at the top of Josh's head.

Ava was taken aback. "No – but I thought I'd show you where the car is?"

They set off over the snow, but the expedition wasn't at all what Ava had expected. Once he was away from Martha, Harry became surprisingly dull. He said almost nothing and paid no attention to her questions. He seemed unfamiliar with both wellington boots and the cold, but at the beginning, Ava forgave him. She found the fact that he didn't want to sledge once they reached the car less forgivable and watched enviously as Josh slid all the way down the hill to the woods.

"Poor Martha," was all Harry said when, after leaning on Ava's shoulder the whole way down the slope, they reached the car. Ava began to wonder if Harry was really the hero he appeared to be.

She watched him unlock the car, reach in and pull out Martha's script, and then dance around flicking lumps of snow from his jacket as if they might contaminate him. Then she had to open the boot for him. He picked out the chocolates and set off up the field without a word. As she slammed the boot shut, she decided that she didn't like him one bit.

"Was it that like that this morning?" asked Josh, panting up the hill for the fourth time, dragging his sledge. He pointed at the rear passenger window, which was smashed in.

"I didn't notice it. Do you think it happened in the accident?"

"We'd have seen it," said Josh. "Wouldn't we?"

Ava stared at it. It was odd, given that the car had just slid over the snow and hadn't actually hit anything. She tried to look through the broken pane, but it was far too high. Whoever broke the window would have been really tall. At least as tall as Harry Hobhouse.

But then Martha had been wearing the necklace after the car accident. Was it the necklace that someone was after? Or something else?

Ava pondered the question all the way up the hill.

CHAPTER 10

Grandpa Edward arrived at the castle to pick up the cousins at the end of the day. After loading the sledges into the back, they made their way slowly in the old Land Rover through the darkness, the headlights flickering on the snowy pillows that lined the road.

"Did you have fun?" asked Grandpa.

"Yes," said Ava. "But I've got a load of words to learn."

"There are secret passages all over the castle," said Chloe.

"And Felicity has a bottomless supply of biscuits," said Josh.

"Well, I've made a roast dinner so hopefully you've still got a bit of room for some potatoes?" said Grandpa.

"Certainly have," said Aiden, rubbing Bella's head. "Certainly have."

"Anyone for sledging?" asked Grandma, after the cousins had eaten their enormous meal.

Chloe really wanted to have a private chat about the necklace with her cousins. She had so many questions. "Could I use your laptop, Grandma, to look up a couple of things? I don't really want to go sledging in the dark."

"It's not literally dark though, is it? Look at that moon." Grandma pointed out of the kitchen window. "It's enormous and the snow's reflecting all the light. But of course you can use the laptop, Chloe, darling – you know where it is. I'm going out in the snow, though."

"Really?" Ava looked shocked.

"Why not?" asked Grandma. "You coming, Edward? Ava? Aiden?"

"Brilliant!" said Josh, running for the back door, jamming his feet into wellies and grabbing his coat as he ran. "Sledging with Grandma!"

"I'm up for it," said Ava, opening the door and searching for wellies.

They all stood at the entrance to the farmhouse, breathing in the crisp, cold air.

For a moment, Chloe hesitated. She looked through the orchard towards the sea. An owl hooted and the moonlight was so strong she could see every detail of the apple trees heavy with snow. In the distance the lighthouse beam bounced off the snow, and below them, the coloured lights of the Drake's Bay Christmas tree finished off the perfect picture. It did look magical.

"Wow," said Aiden, stopping with Chloe to look at the view.

"Look out!" yelled Josh, as he and Ava shot off across the orchard on their sledges.

Chloe looked doubtfully at the sledges left standing against the wall. "What is it you want to look up?" asked Aiden. "Can I help?"

Later, Ava lay in her bed listening to new snow

softly building up on the windowsill outside and smiling about the sledging and the hot chocolate that came afterwards. It was probably the cosiest she had ever felt, ever, anywhere. The room was warm, and painted a lovely blood-orange colour that Grandma had persuaded Grandpa would be just right. The curtains were green velvet and the rug was like a square of bright green grass. If she sat up, she could see over Chloe's bed to the snow that fell steadily, lit by the lamp in the farmyard.

It was like Narnia.

There was a soft knock on the door and Aiden and Josh entered, wearing pyjamas and dressing gowns. They both clambered on to Chloe's bed so that they could watch the snow falling.

Ava looked across at them.

"So?" she said to Aiden. "Why did you and Chloe miss the sledging?"

"Wait a sec," he said. "Chloe?"

Chloe came in from the bathroom wearing a pair of giant rabbit slippers and snuggled into her bed.

Everyone turned to look at her.

"Well?"

Chloe took a piece of paper from her pocket. "This," she said. "It's a not very good drawing, done by me, of Martha's necklace." She held it out towards Josh.

He nodded. "Yup – that just about sums it up."

"OK – now here," she said, holding up Aiden's mobile phone, "is Martha's Uncle Cecil."

Ava peered across the room. There was a man, smiling, about the same age as Grandpa Edward. "So?" she said.

"He's a cousin, lots of times removed, of Queen Elizabeth the First," said Aiden. "He's basically royalty."

"And look." Chloe zoomed in on the photo. "See his neck?"

"It's the same necklace," said Josh. "Almost."

"Why almost?" asked Ava.

"Because the chain's different," said Josh, expanding the picture on the phone. "Look!"

"Can I see?" asked Ava, taking the phone. Josh was correct. This pendant had a fine golden chain with jewels set into it. Not at all like the chain Martha was wearing. But the pendant itself looked exactly the same.

Something chimed in the back of her head. She turned to Josh as he said, "The rear passenger window. The box! And didn't she say something about broken bits of broken bits of other things?"

Chloe gasped. "Do you think the random bits in the box are this chain?"

"It figures," said Ava. "After the accident, after Martha was back at the castle with the necklace and her bags, but before we went down to her car with Harry – someone broke into the car. They were looking for something."

"This chain," said Aiden.

Ava stared at the phone. "Maybe her uncle wears this necklace and the chain breaks. But he puts it in the box anyway."

"Because it's really valuable?" suggested Chloe.

"So the bits of broken stuff are actually this fancy chain," said Josh. "But Martha doesn't know it!"

"Josh," said Aiden. "I think you might possibly be right. We need to find that box."

CHAPTER 11

The next day the Land Rover rattled happily along the road, bursting through snowdrifts and making light work of the ice. Ava stared out of the window at the sunlit countryside. The trees were still heavy with snow, and it was utterly beautiful out there. As Grandpa approached the castle, they passed an orange rescue truck that was pulling Martha's little car up the slope and a few minutes after they arrived, it delivered the car to the castle's driveway.

"Look," said Aiden.

"You can see where the back window's broken,"

said Chloe.

"We need to ask Martha about the box – and is she sure she hasn't got it?" said Aiden.

"We need to search the car properly," said Chloe.

"And we need to search the whole castle," said Josh.

"Like that's going to happen," said his sister. "It's huge."

Inside the castle, Martha was in tears.

"Someone's been in my room!" she sobbed. "They've been through my stuff, Felicity! Someone here has been through my bag. Last night! While I was asleep!"

Ava opened her mouth to ask about the box but stopped herself.

"Oh, Martha," said Felicity. "Surely not. Have you still got your necklace?"

Martha clutched the chain. "Yes, and my rings. It's not that – it's someone going through all my clothes. While I was in bed!"

"Oh dear," said Stanislav. "How awful. But is anything missing?"

Martha did a long sniff and shook her head. "No – I don't think so. It's just…" and she fell into another wave of sobs.

"Are you sure? Have you checked everything?" Ava asked.

"Let's not worry about it now, Ava," said Felicity, whisking Martha away up the stairs. "Let's get your costume sorted instead."

Ava stood at the bottom of the stairs, shaking her head. How on Earth was she going to get a chance to talk to Martha?

Josh and Bella were running. No matter what Ava said, Josh was determined to search the entire castle. Martha's bag being ransacked must mean he was right. It wasn't just the necklace; it was something else as well, and that something else was probably the pieces of the delicate jewelled chain her uncle had been wearing.

He was trying to search all the bedrooms, but Felicity kept on finding jobs for him. Since last night, a load of scenery had appeared, and Josh was tasked with collecting all the missing bits for the team who were putting it up. This was made up of Jeffers, an ancient gardener, and Jake, and Pearl, who ran the kayaks down in Drake's Bay. Finding Aiden holding the bottom of Jeffers' ladder, Josh dumped a load of clips next to him, then ran down to the kitchen to get water for Bella. On his way out, he looked up at the long line of bells on the wall. Twelve bedrooms. How was he ever going to search them all? He'd have to avoid Felicity for long enough to get around the landings. He wondered if she used the passages. Then he wondered if he had the nerve to use the passages on his own. He had Bella, after all. Weren't ghosts afraid of dogs?

On his way up the stairs, he met Robin Baird coming down.

"Found any good routes around the castle recently?" he asked.

Josh shook his head and waited for the man to reach the hall below. He didn't want anyone to see how nervous he was about going in on his own. Feeling his way along the wall, he found a clicky panel and plunged in through the door.

There was no wind and no weird noises. "OK, Bella, we've got this," he said in a confident voice, marching towards the small staircase at the end.

Ignoring all his fears, he clambered up a level until he was pretty sure he was on the landing where the bedrooms ought to be. The passageway was empty, lit only by a very tiny window. A shiver ran down Josh's spine.

"Let's get out of here," he said, suddenly losing his nerve and opening the first door he found. In front of him were clothes and he thought he'd walked into the costume store. "Whoops!" He began to back away from the room and then paused. He looked around at the coat hangers. An orange suit hung against a wardrobe. It was Stanislav's room. A saggy old leather bag lay on the bed and a laptop was on the desk. Yes! He had a chance to search at least one room – and it belonged to one of the main suspects. Thinking ahead, Josh tied Bella to one of the bedposts. "You're going to stay there, Bella. No trouble from you – understand?"

Bella raised an eyebrow, whined and lay down with her jaw resting on her paws.

"Good girl," he said, checking the door and finding it locked. So, only someone with a key could come in that way. He propped open the little door he'd come through so that he'd hear any footsteps approaching and, starting to the left of the window and working his way around the room, he began his search.

Opening every drawer and cupboard and checking under everything took him about five minutes. Finally, he was left looking at the leather bag. He eyed the secret door.

"Gonna have to risk it for the biscuit, Bella."

Carefully, he opened the bag.

CHAPTER 12

"No, no, no!" Stanislav bellowed at Mrs Edge. "You're supposed to be acting! I despair." He pressed the back of his hand to his forehead. Ava assumed they were all supposed to gasp or something, but Stanislav despaired of everything, all the time. He looked around. None of them were paying him any attention. "Anyway," he said. "It's time we stopped for lunch."

Ava had tried to get a moment with Martha all morning – this could be her chance. She was just moving in on the actress when Harry grabbed her for another selfie. Honestly, what had she seen in him? Martha smiled at the camera and then looked down at her chest, her mouth opening in horror.

"It's gone! This time, it's definitely gone!"

"Not the wretched necklace again," sighed Robin Baird from across the room.

"Yes! The wretched necklace!" snapped Martha.

Ava fell to her knees, immediately searching under the chairs in case it had ended up on the floor, but there was no sign. As she looked, she saw Harry Hobhouse reach into his bag, and then glance up. He had a curious expression on his face. Guilt?

"Oh dear," said Felicity with a voice that was starting to creak with a cold. "How tiresome! It must be here somewhere."

"You had it on this morning?" asked Ava.

"Yes, I did. I know I did," Martha said.

"I'll check under the chairs," said Stanislav.

They all checked under the chairs. They all checked inside the chairs. They all checked everywhere.

"It's not here, is it?" said Martha.

Stanislav straightened up. For once, he spoke softly and, Ava thought, looked as if he really cared. "No, Martha dear. I don't think it is."

Josh was holding his breath. This was the kind of thing that Ava usually did, not him, and it was scary. It was doubly scary because the secret corridor door was open and the light was starting to fade and it might be heading for ghost time.

He rummaged through the leather bag. It was in a mess, but he squeezed every item of clothing and shook every sock. He pressed the sides and he decided that there was nothing in there. Next, he turned to the laptop case, which was hanging off the back of a chair. It looked to be empty, the laptop lying on the desk, but again he squished every part of it.

"Ah ha!" he said to Bella, feeling something hand-sized and lumpy in the bottom of the bag. It seemed to be stitched inside, and he was just slipping his fingers between the folds of fabric when the door rattled and he heard the sound of a key in the lock.

Faster than he had ever moved before, Josh

grabbed Bella from her tether and ran for the secret door. He had just made it through when he heard someone heavy stomp into the room.

In the kitchen, Martha was still in tears while she and Felicity peered into her pockets and shook out her trouser legs. Chloe came in with Aiden. They'd been fighting the curtains all morning and she was starving.

"What's happening?"

"It's gone again," whispered Ava.

"When?" asked Aiden.

"Just now," replied Ava, perching her bum on the window ledge. "It just vanished," she whispered. "But," she said, "Harry Hobhouse was acting very suspiciously afterwards. I'd swear he put something in his bag."

"Where's Harry now?" asked Chloe.

"Over there," said Aiden. "They're all in here, except Stanislav. Do you think you could go and have a look in his bag? We can keep him here."

On the other side of the room, Martha's hysteria had reached new heights. "I ought to tell the police," she said. "It's just too much! My necklace, the burglary, the car, my stuff last night, and now the necklace again – oh, I'm so miserable!"

"The police won't want to come out in this, dear," said Felicity, pointing to the window where the snow was collecting on the diamond panes. "And it must be here in the castle somewhere."

"I expect it's in your bedroom," said Mrs Edge, offering Martha another biscuit.

"It isn't – I was wearing it this morning," she snapped.

Chloe watched Ava race off down the corridor and got ready to block the door from the kitchen if necessary.

CHAPTER 13

Although there was no one else in the rehearsal room, Ava pretended to look for her phone. She knew she'd given it to Chloe, but it gave her the excuse to empty her tote bag on the chair next to Harry's bag. If she kept her back to the room, anyone watching would think she was just searching her own possessions. She was eyeing up Harry's bag when the door creaked open. She rushed to the mantelpiece and pretended to look there. It was Robin Baird. He hurrumphed, picked up a newspaper, put it down again and left the room.

"Phew," Ava whispered, tiptoeing back over to Harry's black sports bag. She pulled it alongside her bag and waited, listening, before unzipping it. The zipper seemed far too loud as she drew it back. Pulling the sides apart she peered inside, pulling the contents aside so that she could see properly. There was a neatly folded shirt, a sweater and some hair gel.

"Rats!" she said, poking underneath to find nothing more exciting than a toothbrush. Maybe she had imagined the guilty look? Carefully, she placed the bag back by the chair where she had found it. Listening out for anyone approaching, she whipped Harry's laptop bag out from under the sofa and searched through the zipped compartments, checking each one thoroughly.

Nothing. Not a thing.

Closing each section, she slid it back under the sofa as someone turned the door handle at the end of the room. Ava sprang to her feet and began to plump cushions just as Mrs Edge shuffled back in, holding a costume bag.

"You don't want to do that, lovey," said Mrs Edge. "Why don't you head back to the kitchen.

There's a lovely raspberry sponge."

"Good idea," said Ava, brushing dust from her knees. "See you there."

"When I looked there was nothing there," said Ava.

"So where is it?" asked Chloe.

"In Stanislav's room," said Josh. "I'm sure of it, I just couldn't quite get it in time."

"Possibly," said Aiden. "Let's run through this again." After everyone had finished their pasties and the adults had headed back to the rehearsal room, Felicity had given the cousins a bag of chestnuts. They were attempting to roast them in front of the fire. It hadn't been very successful. One had exploded and three more were burned beyond recognition. Bella had eaten the only one that was probably OK.

"Firstly, Martha has a break-in at home, then someone steals the locket but we find it in the cloakroom. At some point, someone goes to the car and breaks the window, possibly to get − or not get − the box it came in."

"And," said Chloe, "we haven't had a chance to

find out more about the box because we can't get near Martha."

"And now the necklace has disappeared a second time." Aiden peeled shell from a burned lump of chestnut.

"Whoever it was that broke into the car has to be tall," said Ava. "To reach in through that window."

"Or athletic," said Chloe.

"Stanislav," said Aiden. "He's tall, and he came in when we were greeting everyone. He could have gone to the car AND he had something suspicious in his laptop case – such a pity you couldn't get to it, Josh."

Josh kicked at the fireguard. "I know – we need proof."

"It could still be Harry Hobhouse," said Chloe.

"It's not," said Ava.

"And why not? Just because you fancy him," said Josh, "doesn't mean he's not a criminal mastermind."

"I don't fancy him, actually," said Ava. "I think he's a selfish idiot, as it happens. And that's the point. I think he's an idiot. I don't think he'd know anything about the necklace. Whoever has taken it knows there's more to it than we can see hanging around Martha's neck."

Aiden raised his eyebrows. Ava had obviously seriously changed her mind about Harry.

"Anyway. I searched his bag. Nothing," said Ava. "Harry's definitely innocent. I think it's Stanislav."

"Why?" said Chloe.

"What on Earth is he doing here? He's a West End director! This is so lame in comparison to what he normally does," said Ava.

"I don't know," said Aiden. "It could just be that Stanislav is doing a favour for Felicity. She is an old friend, after all. He would want it to be a success for her."

"For all we know, it's Robin Baird," said Josh. "He knows about the passages – and he's definitely not an actor."

"He's also a friend of Felicity's, though," said Aiden. "Some kind of historian."

"Could it be Felicity herself?" said Chloe. "She had every chance and she keeps on finding us things to do, like she thinks we're on to something.

And she knows all the secret passages. Whoever went through Martha's bag this morning probably came in through a secret door."

"Doesn't Felicity just really want the play go well?" said Aiden. "Harry Hobhouse can't take his eyes off Martha."

"But he's in love," said Chloe. "It's different. He's got puppy eyes."

"Hasn't he just," said Ava, sighing. "Such a shame he's a disappointment."

"Ava!" Felicity's call echoed from the rehearsal room. "You're on, dear!"

"Oh – sorry, that's my cue," said Ava. The cousins rose from their chairs and ran to join the rest of the cast, and Ava walked to the side of the stage. Aidan watched as she took a deep breath and stepped through the doorway.

"Hello, everyone," she read from her script. Then for some reason she looked up to the metal bars overhead. Her mouth opened wide in a silent scream and she threw herself at Martha, sweeping her across the stage just as a scaffolding board, attached to a huge piece of scenery, fell in the exact spot where Martha had been standing.

CHAPTER 14

Martha lay on the floor, clinging to Ava, both of them centimetres from the scaffolding board as it skidded to a slow stop.

Aiden and Chloe leapt to help but got tangled with Pearl who'd rushed to do the same.

"What the —?" shouted Stanislav from the side. "What just happened?"

"Are you all right?" asked Ava, sitting up and pulling Martha with her.

"I think so," said Martha in a very small voice, flexing her elbow to see that it was working. "Thank you, Ava."

"My word, that was quick thinking, Ava!" said Felicity, blowing her nose and looking distraught. "So lucky you were there."

"You moved incredibly fast," said a voice from the wings. Chloe couldn't see who it belonged to, but she thought it was Robin Baird.

"I'm wondering if we should call the whole thing off!" said Stanislav, slumping into a chair. "I mean, it's been a catalogue of disasters, hasn't it? We've had one thing after another. The necklace, the car, the snow – perhaps it's just not meant to be, Felicity?"

"Not now, Stanislav," said Felicity. "This show has to go ahead. It raises far too much money to cancel. I really thought Pearl and Jake had the scenery under control."

"Well, so did I," said Pearl. "I can't imagine how it happened. Shocking, absolutely shocking! We only put it up there this morning, and I was sure Jake had tied it on safe as houses."

"Don't look at me," said Jake. "I'm a fisherman – I did proper sailor's knots – proper tight. There was no way they could have come undone. Really, no way. I'll go up and check." He pushed his way through the curtains and a moment later he was up at the top of a long ladder looking at the scaffolding poles.

"I don't understand it," he called. "There's no reason why it should fall, none at all. The bar's steady as a rock. It's not moved an inch."

Below them, Aiden was examining the top of the board that had fallen. In his hands was the thick cord that had been used to attach the board to the scaffolding bars. Chloe looked over his shoulder.

"Look," she said, pointing to the broken end of the cord.

Beside her, Josh yelped. "That's been cut!"

"Jake – when you're down can you look at this?" called Aiden.

When Jake examined the cord, he gasped. "Look here, it's been sawn through." He brandished the cord at the rest of the cast. "This is proper dangerous!"

"I think we should tell the police," said Aiden, immediately turning bright red as everyone in the room stared at him. "There have been a series of events." He swallowed and looked across to Chloe for reassurance. She nodded. "Martha had a car accident, then she lost her necklace, and now the scenery almost falls on her head. Although, it could have fallen on any of you. It's like someone wants to stop the play."

"The children have a point," said Robin Baird. "I mean, isn't this all looking rather ridiculous? Things keep going wrong. Isn't it the fates telling us something? Shouldn't we all pack our bags and say enough is enough?"

"No," said Felicity. "You're all being very defeatist about this – we need to rally, press on, produce the best show we can in the face of adversity."

Robin Baird let out a long sigh, rose from the sofa and walked around the room, but he didn't say anything. Stanislav looked at the ground.

Mrs Edge looked up from her script. "It would be a shame to cancel. I've sold lots of tickets in the village. They're terribly excited to have proper actors. And I think there's been a bake-athon."

"A what?" groaned Stanislav.

"A bake-athon," began Mrs Edge. "It's like a marathon only you bake—"

"We are not cancelling!" squeaked Felicity. She

cleared her throat. "Jake, please can you check every scrap of the scaffolding. It was probably just an old bit of sash cord – we could double up on it if anyone's worried. I really don't think there's anything going on, and the last thing the police need in the middle of this frightful weather is being called out here. Why would anyone want to sabotage the play? And I'm sure the necklace will turn up." Felicity leaned from her end of the sofa to give Martha a hug. Martha blew her nose. This time Aiden leaned over and touched her shoulder.

"Can we ask you a couple of questions in private, Martha?" he whispered.

Martha looked startled. "Can't you ask me here?"

Aiden shook his head and pointed to the back of the great hall.

Martha held her hand up to show five minutes.

Aiden nodded.

"So," said Felicity. "Onwards and upwards! Stanislav – the next scene?"

CHAPTER 15

All four of them waited at the end of the great hall, backs to the room.

"This way," Josh said, "no one can hear or see anything we say."

"I'm wondering," said Chloe, "why anyone would want the play to come to an end now?"

"If they've got the necklace, they'll want to get away. If the play finishes now, they won't be suspected?" suggested Aiden.

"Oh," said Josh. "I get it."

Martha came over, looking exhausted, and

threw herself across three chairs. "What is it?" she groaned.

"You said your necklace came in a box, with some other jewellery?" asked Ava.

"A box?" Martha sat up. "Yes, an odd sort of jewellery box with some random bits and bobs of earrings, I think – why?"

Josh punched the air. The others ignored him. "Do you know where it is?"

Martha looked around; her face wore a puzzled expression. "In my bag – or – no? I don't. Why, do you?"

"We don't, but we're wondering if the random pieces were actually a broken chain," asked Aiden. "Is that possible?"

Martha's expression grew more puzzled. "What do you mean?"

Aiden pulled out his phone and found the picture of Uncle Cecil. "Look, here – see?"

Martha studied the phone and slowly handed it back to Aiden. She nodded as if she was remembering something. "That would figure," she said eventually. "Uncle Cecil inherited all kinds of things from his father – he was an Earl or a Lord.

This necklace might have been part of that." She reached for the phone again and took another look at the picture. "I do remember seeing him wearing the whole thing, but I didn't realise my little pendant and the other pieces were part of it. Do you think he gave me the whole thing but I didn't know it?"

Chloe shrugged. "It would help if you knew where the jewellery box is."

"Hold on a minute," said Martha, now fully awake. "I'll run up to my room and check."

A little later, Martha found Ava and Aiden sorting through costumes upstairs and shook her head.

"No sign?" asked Aiden.

Martha shrugged. "Thin air," she said.

"Could it be in your car?" asked Ava.

"Maybe," said Martha. "Should I check?"

"Don't worry." Ava glanced at Aiden. "We'll do that."

As darkness fell, Chloe slipped out of the kitchen door into the shadowy courtyard. She was armed with Ava's phone torch, Martha's keys, and woolly gloves. The air crackled with cold. She could almost hear the frost forming, but she had a mission. Martha's car was on the other side of the drive, waiting to be taken away when the weather cleared, but it gave Chloe a chance to have a look and see if the box was still there. She clicked the car keys and the locks opened smoothly. She crept inside, shining the torch everywhere, especially at the floor. There was water, and some glass, and then, feeling under the passenger seat, her fingers hit something hard. A box.

Leaning half in, half out of the car she tried to open it but her gloves were thick and her fingers cold. It was promisingly heavy. She bunged it in her pocket and began to climb out of the car.

Clunk.

Footsteps?

She threw herself out of the car and crawled behind another car parked in the courtyard. Light spilled across the courtyard snow and for a second a figure was silhouetted in the doorway. Was it Stanislav? Chloe stayed totally still and watched as the figure crunched over the snow, approaching Martha's car. The feet stopped and someone tried the door. Chloe scrunched herself into the tiniest ball and listened. She heard heavy breathing as the figure reached in, and she heard the sounds of seats sliding back and forth. Then they muttered something, but she couldn't hear the voice properly.

A second later, they crunched over the snow in the direction of a tall pile of garden pots. Whoever it was, there was a rustling sound and then something clanked and she heard the pots grating against each other.

She crouched right down so that she could see underneath the car. A pair of feet stood on the far side and then, to Chloe's great relief, turned and walked back towards the house. She heard the front door shut and allowed herself a long deep breath before rising.

She stood and looked back at the castle. Although yellow squares of light showed at every window, there was no sign of anyone at the doors, and nobody was looking out into the gloom. As quickly as she could, she skirted the car and headed for the piles of garden pots.

She was halfway there ready to see what the noise had been when Grandpa pulled into the drive in the

Land Rover and shouted enthusiastically, "Hello, Chloe! How's it all going? Can we find a cup of tea in Felicity's kitchen?"

He linked his arm in hers and whisked her back towards the steps.

"Hello, Grandpa," she said, wishing he'd arrived five minutes later.

CHAPTER 16

On the way back in the Land Rover, the cousins waited for Grandpa to find a song he liked on the radio and then began to talk quietly among themselves. Chloe pulled the box from her backpack and balanced it on her knee.

It was a tiny set of drawers. Wooden, with patterns cut into it.

"Pretty," breathed Ava.

"Go on. Open it," said Josh.

Shaking her gloves from her fingers, Chloe pulled at the tiny white knob on the front of the top drawer. Inside, lying scattered on purple velvet, lay six pieces of gold, looped at the ends. Each one was studded with a jewel that glinted dully in the light from Aiden's phone. "Emeralds and rubies," whispered Aiden.

Without a word, Chloe opened the second drawer. This one had a short chain of ten golden links. And a long hook, peppered with minute pearls. It was extraordinary. Beautiful.

Chloe pulled open the third drawer. A short piece of gold chain lay there. A flashing green emerald at one end. It all looked really old. Not old and battered, but old and precious.

"Wow," said Josh, picking up one of the jewel-studded links. "This is it, isn't it?"

"You were right, Josh. Martha had the chain all along and didn't even know," said Aiden.

Chloe handed the box to Ava. "And, while I was getting this, I think someone came out to hide the pendant."

"For real?" asked Ava.

"I'm sure I heard someone hide something in the courtyard. But I think the thief is still looking for this," said Chloe. "Someone came out while I was by the car. They opened the door and rummaged under the seats, but I'd already found it. It was in my pocket. At first I thought it was Stanislav, then I was less sure. But whoever it was went to the big pile of plant pots in the corner of the courtyard. He fiddled with it. I heard something make a clink noise."

"Oh, Chloe," said Ava.

"I know, I could have grabbed it right that second, but then Grandpa arrived and I had to go so I couldn't check."

They stared into the box. The pieces of the jewelled chain glinted in the light reflected by the snow.

"Should we get the police now?" said Aiden.

"We should try and find the pendant first," said Josh. "See if it's where Chloe thinks it is."

"And if it is?" said Aiden. "Do we just pick it up and give it back to Martha?"

"No," said Ava. "We see if it's there – and we watch, all the time, to see who goes to find it. Then we call the police. As Felicity says, they won't want to come all the way out here without any evidence."

"But!" Chloe pointed out at the snow and the

darkness outside the windscreen.

"Straight after we've eaten," said Ava. "Are we on?"

"No, Bella, you can't come with us," said Ava, putting two pairs of socks on her feet.

"Wouldn't she be useful?" said Josh.

"She might start barking," Ava replied, unplugging her phone from the charger and zipping it carefully into a pocket. "Ready?"

While their grandparents watched the news, full of apple pie and cream, they crept downstairs. Ava opened the front door and they slipped out into the cold. The moon was out, lighting everything up so clearly that it felt like daylight but without the colour. The snow was crisp under their boots, and they trotted over the surface as quietly as they could. At the first stile, Ava glanced back at the farmhouse. A warm yellow light shone out from her bedroom. She saw Chloe wave and even though they were probably invisible, she waved back.

"I'm already cold," said Josh, hanging back as they launched across the first huge white field.

"Oh, for goodness' sake, Josh, do you want to go

back?" Ava asked. "Chloe was up for it."

"No – it's fine," said Josh.

They stomped across the first field and then began on the second. An owl leapt from a tree and swooped, hooting, over their path. "What was that?" yelped Josh.

"Just an owl."

At the third field, they clambered over a gate and plunged into the woods. They'd only gone a few metres before a startled deer leapt away, crashing through the trees. "Yow!" squeaked Josh, rushing to hold on to his sister's arm. "That made me jump."

Tempting as it was to spook Josh even more, Ava didn't want to jeopardise the mission. Instead, she said, "Not far now. We're almost at the bottom of the sledging hill. Look, there's the castle."

Above them, the old castle walls shone in the moonlight.

"S'creepy," said Josh.

"There are people there. It's not like it's deserted."

"Still creepy," said Josh.

CHAPTER 17

It was easy to get up the field, and within a few minutes they were in the courtyard. Two lights shone in windows at the top of the manor house but the castle towers themselves were eerily dark.

"I'm glad we don't have to go in," whispered Josh. "I bet it's just when the ghosts come out."

They crept across the car park, the frozen snow crunching under their feet. Ava was looking for the pile of flowerpots, but everything had been covered by a fresh layer of snow. Off to her right, she could hear Josh crashing something around.

"Shh," she muttered.

"I think I've – oh!"

"What is it?" Ava tiptoed over, fumbling with her phone until she managed to get the screen to light up just enough to see by.

"Look!"

Ava gasped. "Chloe was right!"

There in Josh's hand was a small plastic bag containing the pendant. "Now what?"

"We can't leave it here, it'll disappear." Ava stared at the necklace. "Come on, let's just go!"

"But I thought we wanted to catch someone picking it up," said Josh.

"Change of plan," she replied. "It's not safe if we leave it here because we can't watch all night long."

"Take it back to the farm?"

"Yup!" She took the bag from Josh and carefully zipped Martha's necklace into the inside of her coat while Josh scattered snow over the flowerpots.

"Ready?" he whispered.

Ava nodded. "Time to go," she said.

Which was when Ava suddenly became aware of the castle door opening.

She shrank down, pulling Josh with her until they were wedged between two cars, hardly daring to breathe.

She watched as a figure in black moved across the car park through the shadows. A torch came on. The figure was definitely looking for something. Ava felt the lump of the pendant against her side. They needed to get away.

And fast.

If they were quick, they would be able to get around the car park without being spotted. Keeping her head down, Ava scuttled away from the figure and the plant pots. She was aware of Josh panting behind her. It sounded far too loud, but she didn't dare speak.

They reached the edge of the cars but there was a huge empty space that they needed to cross before they could disappear into the snow beyond the castle.

Josh crouched beside her, and Ava risked a look towards the figure who still appeared to be searching. Although she couldn't see any details, she could see the height, and this person wasn't tall enough to be Stanislav. Too tall to be Mrs Edge.

Who did that leave?

"C'mon," said Josh, at her side. She watched as Josh straightened a little and, staying close to the ground, loped across the open space and vanished into the snow beyond. The searching person didn't seem to notice. They were shaking plant pots and making quite a lot of noise.

"OK," said Ava to herself, and she ran into the darkness, expecting someone to shout her name at any moment.

Josh waited in the hedge until he could see Ava.

"We did it!" he hissed and high-fived his sister. "Yay!" He jumped in the air and landed, missing his footing and sliding down the slope.

"Run, run!" squeaked Ava, and she shot past, bouncing and falling and shooting snow into the air in her wake. Josh scrambled to catch up, and together they half-skidded, half-ran into the woods, sending startled pheasants screaming from their roosts.

"Do you think he saw us?" said Josh, pausing for breath.

"Or she," said Ava. "No – I think we probably got away with it." They both looked up the hill towards the castle. It was silent. No one was looking down on them. Ahead of them were the spooky woods. Josh swallowed. Was it better to send Ava first, or have her at his back? But before he could adopt a strategy, Ava shouted, "There's someone coming!" and took off through the trees.

Fear made Josh run faster and so it took them only a few minutes to run deep into the woods. And only a few seconds for Josh to lose Ava altogether.

He froze. He couldn't possibly call out to Ava. Not if there was someone after them.

Moving as slowly as he could, he stopped with his back to a tree and looked up the slope. Whoever had followed them had disappeared. Or they were hiding.

He swung round and stared through the trees. A snowflake landed on his nose and he realised that the moonlight had gone, that heavy clouds now covered the sky and that snow was beginning to fall.

"Ava?" he cried. "Ava – where are you?"

CHAPTER 18

Aiden sat on Chloe's bed and together, they waited. He knew the plan was that they would take it in turns to watch where the necklace was hidden, but he also knew it wouldn't work. It was too cold. Middle of summer might have been OK, but not now, not in a snowstorm. When Ava and Josh had left, everything was clear and moonlit, but now, the snow was falling again and it looked really cold out there. "They ought to be back by now," said Chloe.

Aiden nodded. He glanced at his phone. It was

past midnight. "I expect they're taking the long way back," he said, not believing himself at all.

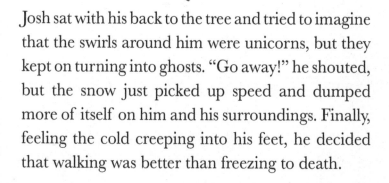

Ava stopped, sucking in lungfuls of air, and looked back for Josh.

He wasn't there. "Josh?" she called quietly through the thickly falling snow. "Josh?"

She had a sudden image of trying to explain this to Grandma. It would not go down well. She turned and, placing her boots carefully in her own footsteps, threaded her way back through the trees. The wind blew hard in her face, the snow blinded her, and within minutes she came to the awful realisation that her footprints were disappearing.

"Josh?" she called into the blizzard. "Josh?"

Josh sat with his back to the tree and tried to imagine that the swirls around him were unicorns, but they kept on turning into ghosts. "Go away!" he shouted, but the snow just picked up speed and dumped more of itself on him and his surroundings. Finally, feeling the cold creeping into his feet, he decided that walking was better than freezing to death.

He tried to work out which direction he'd come from, but the snow cut everything off. He looked at his boot prints but the ones that hadn't been obliterated pointed in all directions.

"Ava!" he shouted, breaking a stick from a tree and using it to prod the ground in front. "Ava! Where are you?"

Chloe woke from a doze and realised it was hours later. She saw that Aiden was asleep on Ava's bed. She reached over and tugged at his elbow. "They're not back and look, it's snowing even harder."

They sat for a minute staring out of the window. "Let's go and find them," said Aiden eventually.

They crept down through the sleeping house, past Bella's snoring and out through the front door, stopping only to take a front door key.

"Keep together, yeah?" said Aiden, pulling his hat down over his ears, and Chloe nodded agreement.

They set off the way they'd seen Ava and Josh leave hours earlier, but there were no footprints to follow, none at all, and Aiden struggled to see where they were going. At first, they walked to the edge of the woods. Then as far as the bottom of the hill leading up to Frost Castle. They walked for so long that the snow stopped and the moon came out.

"Josh!"

"Ava!"

"Josh!"

"Ava!"

Eventually Aiden looked at his phone. "Five AM," he said. "I can't imagine where they are."

"I'm so tired," said Chloe. "Maybe they slept at the castle."

Aiden gazed at the woods, the thick snow reaching on and on. "This is hopeless," he said. "Let's go back to bed and check when it's light. I think you're right, they've gone back to the castle."

They turned and began to head back, tramping through the knee-deep snow. It was hard going and before long the moonlight disappeared and the snow began to fall again.

Aiden stopped to clear the snow from his glasses. "Are you sure we're heading the right way?" he asked when he put them back on. "It's just the slope of the hill seems to be going the wrong way."

"Oh no," said Chloe, turning in a circle. "We're lost!"

Josh plodded on. He couldn't see much, and he was incredibly hungry. He was hallucinating pancakes and chocolate sponge and fried chicken to the point where he almost cried. He was just imagining a warm salty bowl of rice and peas when he came across a pile of thick brushy branches. "Oooh!" he said, tugging at the end of one of them. It shot out and bounced across the ground, spraying him with snow. Underneath it were masses more, all thick, and the lower ones were actually quite dry. Putting down his stick, he took the longest branches and, tepee style, leaned them against a straight tree trunk. Then, he took the dryer ones and layered them inside. Finally, he crawled in, held his walking stick close, and after about two minutes of imagining bears and ghosts, fell soundly asleep.

Ava wasn't in a total panic, just a kind of half panic. She had followed her footsteps as far as she could and she'd had to take shelter from a violent ten minutes of snowfall, which meant she lost the last few metres of her own track. Taking what she hoped was a direct line towards the castle, she trekked on, and then, after what seemed like hours, found Josh's prints.

"Hurrah!" she shouted and turned to follow them. They were quite clear, and he seemed to have developed an extra very small foot that made it easier to find. He had however wandered in circles, and she was concentrating so hard on working out which direction he was going in she missed the pile of branches on the side of the path. The tracks stopped. Quite suddenly.

Had he been taken by some flying creature? She stamped about and searched in every direction. "Josh?" she called. "Josh?"

"Ava?" came a voice from right beside her. "You took your time!"

CHAPTER 19

Chloe was actually asleep on her feet by the time she'd located the farm. It was the distant beam of the lighthouse that led them in the right direction and they didn't even say a word to each other as they slipped back into the house. Aiden crawled off to sleep in his bed and Chloe, expecting to go to sleep instantly, climbed into hers. But she didn't sleep. Instead, she stared out of the window, willing her cousins to appear. At half past seven, after she'd heard her grandparents getting up, Aiden knocked on the door.

"Couldn't sleep," he said.

"There they are," said Chloe, pointing.

Aiden peered. "Thank goodness!" Ava and Josh were almost snowmen out there in the dark, lurking at the edge of the garden.

"How are they going to get back in? Grandma'll spot them a mile off."

"Diversion?" Aiden said.

"OK," Chloe agreed. "Tummy ache?"

Leaving the lights off, they crept from the bedroom and slipped noiselessly downstairs. Aiden opened the catch on the front door while Chloe bent over and clutched her stomach, letting out a moaning sound.

Aiden shook his head. "Not very convincing – more moan, less squeak?"

"Oooh, Grandma," said Chloe, stepping up the volume. "My stomach really hurts." Slipping Aiden a quick smile she opened the kitchen door and went in, closing it behind her.

"Oooh, ow – it really hurts."

He could hear the moaning and concerned Grandma sounds: "Oh, my love!" and "Try a hot water bottle."

And then someone ran a tap and the pipes clanked. Tiptoeing, Aiden reached for the front door and pulled it open. Immediately, Bella woke from her bed in the hall and let out a single bark.

"In, in!" he hissed to the two figures outside. Ava and Josh rushed past and raced straight up the stairs in their snowy boots, scattering chunks of snow all over the place. "Bella, here!" Aiden called Bella over and threw a ball out into the snow. Bella leapt, raced around in the snow, sniffed the air and galloped back in, bringing a large quantity of snow with her that she distributed around the hall. "Yay! Good dog!" he said, picking up the biggest lumps of ice and chucking them out through the door.

"Oh, Bella!" said Grandpa, checking to see what the noise was.

"I just let her out for a wee and she brought all this snow back in with her!"

"Good lad, Aiden. You go back to bed, I'll sort this out."

"Is Chloe OK?" asked Aiden.

"Oh she'll be fine, just too many pasties, I suspect. You go back up to bed. Have another half hour."

He left his grandfather chasing lumps of ice

around the floor with Bella. On the way up the stairs, he scooped up all the obvious snow and ran to his bedroom, where Josh stood in his T-shirt and pants, waving his coat and boots out of the window.

"Freezing," said Josh.

"What happened?" asked Aiden.

"We got it! Meeting in five."

They gathered on Chloe's bed. Ava clutched Chloe's hot water bottle. Chloe eyed a peppermint tea with disgust.

"Here," said Ava, placing the necklace and the broken chain on the bed. They lay there, rich, golden and beautiful on the coverlet.

"Wow!" said Chloe. "I can totally see that they belong together – this chain is just rubbish compared to the real one." She undid the necklace and slid the pendant off, holding it next to the pieces of the jewelled chain.

"It's really old," said Aiden, lifting off his glasses and peering at it up close.

"I'm sure it's a locket," said Chloe. "But I couldn't work out how to open it. Aiden?"

Aiden held it about five centimetres from the end of his nose. "I see what you mean. It ought to open down the side here. So, did you see anyone?"

"Yes," said Josh. "A person came to pick it up, or look for it."

"Stanislav?" asked Chloe.

"No – they weren't tall enough," said Ava. "It might even have been a woman. We ran – we didn't hang around to have a look. I was expecting someone to come in a car. Not walk out of the castle."

"A woman?" Chloe accidentally sipped her peppermint tea. "Yuck!" She watched Aiden fiddling with the necklace as everyone discussed all the people who could possibly be involved.

And then something occurred to her. "Pull the little pin up – at the top, where it comes down from the chain."

"What – here?" said Aiden, pinching the top link between his thumb and his forefinger. Chloe bit her lip as he pulled. It was the only way she could possibly imagine that the thing would open.

"Ah," said Aiden, as his fingernails gripped the pin. "It's coming out."

Chloe moved so close her nose was practically touching Aiden's.

"Yes!" she said as the pin came out, and the pendant fell open in Aiden's hand. Inside was a tiny, perfectly painted portrait of a woman. Even though it was miniscule, Chloe could see every pearl in her hair, every spot of blush on her cheek. It was the most beautiful thing she'd ever seen. "Wow!" She breathed. "That's stunning!"

"Can I see?" asked Ava, taking it from Aiden and holding it under the light. "Whoa! That's amazing. Who do you think she is?"

Aiden reached for his phone. "I've seen something like this before in a museum – it's called a miniature, I think."

"It's certainly very small," said Ava. "Do you think it's really precious?"

Aiden didn't answer. He was looking something up on his phone. "Let's just have another look," he said.

Ava held it in front of his face and glanced across at his phone. "Oh, Aiden – that's just like it. Who is that woman on there?"

There was a long silence while Aiden looked back

and forth from the locket to the screen. "Surely not," he said in the end.

"Not what?" said Josh. "Is she famous?"

"It's … Queen Elizabeth the First." Aiden put down his phone and swept his fringe back. "It looks just like this one. Painted by a bloke called Nicholas Hilliard. It's, like, the most valuable thing, ever – it should probably be in a museum, and we just stopped it from being stolen!"

CHAPTER 20

"So, today is the dress rehearsal and then it's the performance tonight. It feels like we're not remotely ready but there's nothing much we can do about that," said Felicity, blowing her nose. Josh looked up at her. The end of her nose was a total balloon and her eyes were watering, and she was kind of wobbly. Josh assumed she'd caught Martha's cold. Mrs Edge was also sniffing and dabbing at her face with a large white handkerchief. "Josh – can you do the prompt, please?"

He'd been doing it yesterday. Then, it was a

boring job; today, it gave him the chance to observe all the actors close up. He was trying to read their behaviour, see who was most flustered, although that was tricky as none of them knew their lines. Sometimes, Robin would forget a whole chunk and Josh found huge delight in reminding him painfully of every line, or Felicity would go down in a coughing fit and flap her hand towards him. At that point, Josh would take the stage – performing the part of Aunt Maud to, he thought, perfection.

The problem was that Martha was on stage practically the whole time so she was never alone. Ava was supposed to tell her about how they'd recovered the necklace and that it was worth a fortune, but so far she hadn't had a chance. Ava was one hundred per cent correct; Harry spent far too much time staring at Martha. Every time she sat down, he jumped to sit by her side.

Perhaps he thought she was an amazing actress.

One thing that wasn't amazing was the play. Ava's lines were truly woeful, so bad that Josh was tempted to record them so that he could play them back to her later. And some of it was definitely more of a comedy than a murder mystery, but Josh thought that was probably accidental.

Just now, Robin and Martha were doing a scene. She was draped over a strange sofa that pointed in two directions and he was pacing back and forth behind her.

Felicity drooped over another chair. Almost asleep.

"So, Dale, darling, will you play tennis with me this afternoon?" said Martha, looking up at Robin.

"Oh," said Robin. "I don't know, tennis bores me frightfully."

"Does it, my sweet?" said Martha, sucking in her cheeks and making her eyes bigger.

Josh looked over to Felicity. It was her line, but her eyes were shut.

"Felicity," called Stanislav. "Felicity – DARLING! WAKE UP!"

"So sorry, Stanislav," said Felicity, standing up. "What am I saying? Oh dear…" She put her hand to her forehead and began to sway.

Josh watched her tip and although he sprang to his feet, and Ava and Harry jumped to theirs, none of them got there before Felicity fell heavily to the floor.

"Oh no!" shouted Ava.

"For goodness' sake," sighed Robin.

"Robin!" said Martha. "Poor Felicity. She must be really unwell."

Josh peered past Martha. He was relieved to see there wasn't any blood or anything, but Felicity was sheet white and although her eyes were open now, it didn't look as if she was focussing on the faces leaning over her. Ava ran off to get a glass of water while Harry and Martha helped her to sit upright.

"This is the final straw," muttered Stanislav.

"Oh dear, oh dear." Felicity tried to get up but flopped back down, despite Martha and Harry's attempts to keep her upright. "I really, I really…"

"Stay where you are," said Martha.

"Yes," agreed Harry. "I think you need to stay put, and I don't know what we're going to do about your part." He looked over to Mrs Edge, who was licking the chocolate off the top of a biscuit and seemed to show no interest in what was going on at all.

"We'll have to cancel the whole thing," said Robin Baird. "You can't have a murder mystery without a body."

"Agreed," said Stanislav.

"We can't cancel it," murmured Felicity. "The show must go on!"

Josh silently agreed. Until they'd worked out who'd stolen the necklace, they had to keep all the suspects there. And then he had a thought. A genius, wonderful thought. Or was it a stupid thought? It didn't matter, he was going to say it anyway.

"I could do it."

"What?" said Martha and Harry together.

"I could do Felicity's part," he said. "I practically know it already. Listen…" Clearing his throat, Josh summoned up his poshest, plumiest accent: "I cannot believe that young people nowadays no longer wish to play tennis like they used to in my youth." He emphasised the "oo" in "youth", and looked around for approval. Stanislav's mouth hung open, Martha's eyes were wide and Ava, who had arrived back with the water, had a huge grin on her face.

CHAPTER 21

It gave Ava the chance she needed. While Josh was being readied for performance by Diedre de Lhonghi, the costume woman, Ava managed to get Martha into the bathroom, figuring it was the only place Harry wouldn't follow her.

"We've got it back!" she said, as Chloe and Aiden joined them.

"What? Why didn't you say so?" said Martha.

"Because, no matter what you say about the rest of the cast, one of them is a thief – but we don't know who, and we don't have any proof. We need to catch them at it. Have you got it, Chloe?

"Lock the door," whispered Chloe, reaching into her backpack and pulling out a t-shirt. She unfolded the t-shirt and laid it flat in the bottom of the basin. On the top she placed the pendant and the pieces of the jewelled chain.

"Oh! It's beautiful – amazing," said Martha. "But where did the other chain come from? Is that mine too?"

"It was the broken pieces in the box," said Ava.

"And," said Aiden. "We're sure the pendant is much, much more valuable than you think. We believe it's an Elizabethan miniature. Look inside."

"Elizabethan – as in Queen Elizabeth – Shakespeare, all that?"

Aiden nodded.

"Wow." Martha ran her fingers over the jewels. "How come? How do you open it?"

"Like this," said Aiden, pulling the pin and opening the pendant.

"Oh my days!" said Martha, looking at the picture. "Who's that? What's she doing in my necklace?"

"We think the woman could be Queen Elizabeth herself," said Chloe. "She used to get little paintings of herself done and give them to her favourite people. This could be one of those."

"Gosh," said Martha, sitting back and looking at her necklace. "This totally explains everything that's been happening. The burglaries, the break-ins. Why didn't Uncle Cecil tell me it was so special?"

"Perhaps he thought he had," said Aiden. "If you look at pictures of him, he's always wearing it. It was obviously important to him."

Martha held one of the jewelled pieces to the light. It glowed green. "I think he inherited it. I think it's always been in the family, but I had no idea – I thought it was Victorian or something." She sat back on the ground. "But who would steal it – are they really a bunch of thieves?"

"Well, one of them must be," said Ava. "We saw someone last night. They'd hidden the pendant in the car park."

"Who?" said Martha.

"That's what we don't know. We need to catch them trying to get it back."

"Gosh," said Martha, dangling both parts of the necklace from her wrist. "What a thing. So how do we keep it safe and find out who was trying to steal it? Any ideas?"

Ten minutes later, Josh joined the rehearsals. It made it much funnier, but not perhaps what Stanislav had in mind. Diedre de Lhonghi, the costume woman, had looked at Josh with horror but cut half a metre off the bottom of Felicity's dress there and then. "Really?" she said, her mouth full of pins.

"And then if I just stuff cushions under here," said Josh, filling the dress front and back and pulling a belt tight around the middle. "I'll look the part, won't I, Ava?"

Ava did her best not to laugh at the look on Stanislav's face, but it was superb. "Josh — Josh," said the director. "This is not a pantomime. This is a serious piece of avant-garde drama. Look at the set — does that say pantomime to you? Does it?"

Ava glanced at the set. It didn't say pantomime, but then it didn't say anything else much. She looked at the clock. Right now, Aiden and Chloe were trying to persuade the bedridden Felicity that one of her actors was a thief and they were asking to borrow a piece of her jewellery to use instead of the necklace. Ava only hoped it would work. Josh was supposed to be distracting everyone. In fairness, he was doing a terrific job.

He and his extra cushions continued to strut about and Stanislav continued to fume. Then Josh went too far.

Ava was about to give Mrs Edge her line, when she broke down in giggles at Josh's antics. Stanislav threw down his script, let out a full-throated scream and turned to face Josh. "This is impossible. Here I am, Stanislav Jones, feted by the West End, darling of New York and Paris, reduced to directing this – this sham, this Aunt Sally of a production. And then, I get you – idiot CHILD! How can I hold my head up? I know it's the first performance tonight. I know the stakes are high. I know that the world's eyes will be upon me, but I'm sorry everyone, I quit!"

This was not part of the plan.

"No! He's going to get away," said Chloe, coming back into the hall carrying a hastily put together necklace made from some of Felicity's eccentric jewellery collection. She rushed to hang the fake around Martha's neck. "Josh, you've gone too far. Martha, you've got to make him stay, he'll get away."

Grabbing a silk scarf to disguise the fake necklace, Martha leaped off the stage to plead with Stanislav but he was too angry to calm down, insisting that Felicity should drive him to the station as she had involved the "awful children" in the first place. Felicity refused, and Stanislav stomped up and down the corridors slamming doors and throwing a tantrum. Chloe glanced at Martha's neck. The fake was just visible under the scarf. Perfect.

"I must have a taxi!" demanded Stanislav.

"I'll call one," said Aiden. He went through the motions. Pretending to dial, pretending to speak, listen and then telling Stanislav, "They can't guarantee anything – they'll come if they can." As he ran up the stairs, Chloe gave him a thumbs up.

A little later, effectively trapped in the castle, Stanislav retired to his room. "Tell me if they arrive. I'll take no part in this travesty."

Finally, the rehearsal began again. It definitely wasn't what Stanislav had had in mind, but it was more fun. Jeffers was now the prompt, and Jake from the village had taken on Stanislav's part, but he was not a natural actor. Felicity crawled out of bed and lay across three chairs, blowing her nose on a more or less continuous basis and throwing suggestions at the actors. Her voice had practically disappeared.

"Jake, darling, try and feel the part a little," she croaked. "You're a rich uncle, not someone the cat brought in."

"Righty ho, Fliss," said Jake, straightening himself and delivering his lines in exactly the same way as before.

Off to the side, Robin Baird let out a long sigh, and Harry Hobhouse sat with his head in his hands.

Chloe and Aiden watched from the balcony. No one was taking the bait, even though Martha fiddled with the borrowed locket around her neck from time to time, letting the light catch it.

Maybe she was being too obvious. Chloe chewed her lip and imagined every possible way in which someone could take the necklace. But all of them would be in plain sight and maybe that was the point. There were too many witnesses for someone to take it. They wouldn't try now. They'd try out of shot somewhere. Hmmm. That meant they needed to keep Martha under observation the whole time.

Chloe began to relax, and fiddled with the sound board. Alongside her, Aiden took careful note of every little change in the lighting. "Can you slide this one up and this one down?" he asked Chloe, pointing at the lighting board. She moved into his chair and tried to do exactly what he wanted.

Which was when everything kicked off.

CHAPTER 22

Josh was standing on the stage. He wore Felicity's cut-down dress and was twice his normal width because of the extra enormous cushion he'd rammed into the bodice. In fact, it was so jammed with cushions now, he could hardly breathe and had broken out into a sweat. He was just adjusting the belt that held it all together when Martha let out a cry.

"Nooo!" she yelled. "Stop him!"

Josh looked up to see Robin Baird leap from the back of the stage to the floor before disappearing into the wall.

"What?" Josh paused, staring at the rest of the cast.

"He took the necklace!" shouted Ava. "After him!"

She tore past and charged though the door in the wall that led to the secret passages.

Finally understanding what had happened, Josh dropped the teacup he was holding and ran to follow, only slightly jamming in the doorway as he tried to catch up with Ava. "Stupid cushions!" he shouted, flinging them backwards into the hall.

"Mind what you're doing!" shouted Jake, but Josh didn't bother to apologise, he just ran on into the corridors behind.

Immediately, he stopped at a junction. "Which way?" he said, listening for footsteps. But the footsteps seemed to be coming from all directions.

"Hey! Ava!" he yelled, pausing for a reply. Off to his right he could hear someone getting closer, to his left, it sounded like they were running away.

Josh ran ten paces one way, then turned and ran ten paces the other way. As he ran, he realised one thing. He needed a weapon. What good would it be if he met Robin Baird in a passage and couldn't stop him?

He charged back out of the door, to see Harry Hobhouse flapping a piece of paper at Martha as if she'd fainted. "Yuck," muttered Josh and, grabbing a walking stick that Felicity had used as a prop, he charged back through the hole in the wall, this time determined to turn left.

As he thundered down the narrow passage, the walking stick in his hand, he heard feet pounding in the passage behind him; still running, he looked back over his shoulder.

"Chloe! Aiden!" he panted.

"You go right!" yelled Chloe. "I'll go left with Bella, hopefully we can cut him off!"

"I'll follow you, Josh!" shouted Aiden and they peeled off along another passage, leaving Chloe to charge off the other way. In step, they bounced along the passage until they came to the spiral staircase. "I'll go up," shouted Josh and he charged up the first few steps, listening for the sound of feet.

There was nothing, and within ten steps Josh

was feeling creeped out again.

By eleven, it felt horribly spooky. He remembered Lady Anne. It was New Year. He hadn't seen her so far but…?

A super-cold breeze flickered over his skin.

He stopped running.

Above him, something howled, a gust of freezing wind shook the fringe of Felicity's dress and a door slammed shut.

"Ava?" he called, so quietly she couldn't possibly hear. "Ava – are you up there?"

Ava did not have a weapon. She had nothing at all except for a phone, and she couldn't get a signal. She didn't know her way around the passages and was utterly confused about where she was. Staircases had emerged on both sides of her, but she'd followed Robin Baird halfway up one of the two big stone towers and now she'd lost him. It was cold up here. There was snow blowing in through the windows but not so much snow that she could see any footprints. She didn't know if there was any other way out, or just the staircase. Was he trapped at the top or had he found another passage?

Listening until her ears rang, she began to shake from the cold. This was mad. She needed to move, one way or the other. She risked another three steps, listened, and again heard nothing. Two more. Stop, listen.

In front of her was a tiny landing with a door, but the steps went on up. Ava hesitated, wondering which way to go. If she stayed where she was, she could stop him running down the stairs, but if she stayed where she was she would also freeze to death.

She was still trying to work out what to do, when the door swung open releasing a howling wind. Bursting in with a blast of snow, Robin Baird swept past her. Ava tried to go for his legs but he was too strong and swatted her out of the way.

"Hey!" she shouted, grabbing at his coat, getting hold of his sleeve. "Don't you dare!"

But he slipped out of the coat, leaving it hanging in Ava's hands, and charged past her, rattling down the stairs while she was still trying to get her balance.

CHAPTER 23

Aiden stopped at the very bottom of the spiral staircase in what he thought was the more crumbled of the two towers. There was no way out down here. Robin Baird couldn't possibly have come this way. Just to make sure, Aiden shook the grille that led out into a kind of mossy dark dungeon space. It stayed rock solid. He turned and made his way slowly back up the spiral staircase, checking for secret doors or windows that might possibly provide an escape. He was nearly back at the landing when he heard shouts from above.

"No!" It was Josh's voice.

"Get out of my way, you wretched child!"

"No, I won't." There was a sound like wood bashing on stone.

"You little toe-rag!"

"Just because I'm small doesn't – ow!"

"Josh?" Aiden ran towards the sound. "Josh?"

Aiden got to within sight of Josh's legs when Robin Baird leapt into view, brandishing a walking stick.

"You going to stop me?" he challenged as he ran towards Aiden.

For a second Aiden thought he might be able to stop him, but then worked out that the man was at least twice his weight. At the last second, Aiden dodged, let the man charge past, and set off in pursuit.

From a passage on the right, a white ball of fur emerged. It was Bella, her paws clattering on the stone as she barrelled towards Aiden, leaping and barking.

"Stupid creature!" shouted Robin Baird, jumping over Bella and just missing Chloe, who stuck her hand out to stop him and got slapped away.

"Get him!" yelled Aiden, skipping past Chloe and braking hard on the next corner. He needed to keep Robin in sight, but the guy was so fast on his feet and unfortunately Bella was determined to keep pace. Aiden slipped.

"Ow!" he shouted as he skidded into the wall.

"Look!" Chloe overtook him. "He's gone up to the Minstrels' Gallery. Cut him off – go out through there." She pointed to a door in the wall and Aiden ran straight through into the rehearsal room. Swerving around Mrs Edge, who was tidying away coffee mugs and didn't seem to have noticed there was a high-speed chase going on, he charged out into the hall and then on into the Great Hall.

There, up in the gallery, was Robin Baird.

Harry Hobhouse appeared, out of breath, from the hall. "You can't get away!" he shouted. "Give back the necklace – hand yourself in."

"Wanna bet?" yelled Robin, and he ducked back into the gallery, disappearing from sight.

As Chloe crept through the hole that led from the passage to the gallery, she held Bella back by her side, but something didn't feel right. It was too cold. There was a freezing wind.

"What?" She stuck her head out of the hole and looked along the gallery. There, where there should have been a chunk of wall, was snow. Falling snow. Lots of it.

She ran to the entrance and looked out. There was the courtyard, and a narrow flight of stone steps, with Robin Baird nearly at the bottom.

"There's another door! He's there!" she shouted as Ava and Josh crashed into the gallery to join her.

"No!"

"After him!" yelled Ava.

The four of them piled down the steps, Josh tripping over the dress, Ava tripping over Bella and Chloe aware that she was only wearing a sweatshirt and trainers and that the snow was freezing.

Ahead of them, Robin Baird skidded over the courtyard, heading for the cars.

"Quick, Josh, block the entrance," muttered Ava. Chloe grabbed Josh by the elbow and they ran together towards a pile of snow that she knew was really a stack of firewood. She was vaguely aware of a commotion to her right as Aiden burst from the main doors of the castle. He was followed by Harry Hobhouse, who immediately turned on his heel and rushed back inside.

"Yay!" shouted Josh next to Chloe, surprisingly unhampered by the enormous dress dripping off his shoulders. "If you kick them, they roll."

Together they pulled out two of the largest logs and scrabbled to heave them into the gateway of the courtyard, kicking smaller ones out into the gaps as they did so.

"Ow!" Ava shouted. Chloe looked round. Robin Baird was trying to get into a car, but Ava and Aiden were making it hard. Ava was whacking him on the back of the legs with a branch and Aiden kept lunging for the car keys.

"You stupid kids!" he shouted, slamming the car door. He brushed past them and leapt over the logs towards the lane outside.

Bella gave chase and the rest of them followed, fanning out across the lane and sliding and tripping through the thick snow.

"Where can he go?" yelled Aiden.

"To the village?" answered Ada.

"He'd never make it!"

At which point, Robin Baird vaulted over a gate to the left and doubled back along the other side of the hedge.

Josh slid to a halt and began to run back the way they'd come. He knew he couldn't beat a fully-grown man over the lumpy fields, but he reckoned he'd be faster on the road. Beside him panted Chloe, and step for step they ran back towards the castle, although he was also aware of someone else running parallel behind the hedge.

Far ahead of them, Robin Baird shot out into the lane.

"Oh no!" Josh shouted.

"I don't think I can go any faster," Chloe mumbled.

Josh felt the same. His sides hurt. He was getting a stitch, he was boiling, the snow stung his face but didn't make him any cooler, and Robin Baird was getting away.

CHAPTER 24

Aiden watched in horror as Robin Baird, far ahead of them, pushed the logs out of the castle gateway and headed back to his car.

Distantly, the courtyard rang with the revving engine.

"No!" shouted Ava and they pounded back on to the lane, neck and neck with Chloe and Josh, all of them running flat out, Bella bounding and bouncing and totally getting in the way.

"Cut him off!"

Josh and Chloe stopped by the gateway and

began to throw snowballs at the car, which reversed, skidded and headed straight for them.

"Windscreen!" yelled Chloe and beside her, Josh threw snowballs as fast as he could, completely covering the windscreen.

The car slid into the wall.

"We've stopped him!" shouted Aiden, and the four cousins formed a snowball line, waiting for the man to get out of his car.

It took a few moments, then he sprang out as if he was going to make another run for the lane, but Aiden and Ava headed him off, driving him back towards the castle walls.

"Keep throwing!" shouted Ava, and Chloe ran for the cars, scooping huge handfuls of fresh snow into tight balls and flinging them at the snow-covered figure.

"Stop! Stop!" shouted Robin Baird. "I give in!"

"Kids! I'll get him! Let me!" yelled a voice from the castle steps. A man appeared, holding a long spear from one of the suits of armour in the hall.

"Harry Hobhouse?" said Josh in disbelief. And next to him, Martha.

"Get him!" shouted Aiden, ignoring Harry

completely, and the cousins closed in, trapping Robin against the castle wall, where Harry Hobhouse, when there was absolutely no danger of Robin getting away, jumped on him, squashing him into the snow.

"I got him," he said triumphantly, holding the spear in one hand and taking a selfie with the other.

It was only a few minutes later that the first people arrived from the village, and the castle, which moments before had been the site of a high-speed chase, began to fill with people expecting to see a play.

The cast assembled in the rehearsal room. Robin Baird, held at spearpoint by Josh, glowered at them all.

"Well, put him somewhere safe!" squeaked Mrs Edge. "After all, he's a criminal! A thief!"

"Yeah, yeah," said Harry Hobhouse, sweeping the flop of his fringe back over his head. "Definitely be a waste of my efforts to let him go again. Let's ask Felicity if there's a safe room or something. And Martha, darling – I got your necklace back." Harry handed Martha the locket, taking slightly too long to let go of it.

Ava caught Josh giving Harry a look of disgust and had to stifle a giggle.

"Oh Harry, thank you so much," Martha smiled. "This isn't actually the real one. Aiden's got that safe. Haven't you?" She fluttered her eyelashes at Aiden.

Aiden turned red.

Chloe mimed being sick.

Ava let her giggle turn into a prolonged cough, and Felicity rose from a sofa and scowled at Robin Baird.

"I'm appalled. Simply appalled," she squeaked, her voice painfully hoarse. "Now what are we going to do? We have a play, we have an audience. We can't have policemen in the middle of it. It wouldn't do at all."

"Is there a dungeon?" asked Aiden. "We could call the police and they could come later on."

"Oh, darlings," said Felicity. "It's rather spidery, but…" She beamed. "It would serve him right."

Ava, Aiden and Felicity marched Robin Baird

through a dark metal-studded door that led from the kitchen.

"Now, there are no secret tunnels out of here, you awful man," said Felicity, opening another smaller door. "It's my grandmother's pantry — she used to keep preserves in here. If you're lucky, there might still be the odd pickled egg."

"I demand my rights!" said Robin Baird. "This is false imprisonment."

"No, it isn't," said Felicity. "You should be grateful I haven't thrown you from the castle walls. That's what my forebears would have done." She closed a metal grille and shot a bolt across. "You've utterly betrayed my trust. I thought you were an academic."

"I am," he said. "An impoverished academic."

"Well, I think you're an absolute rotter," said Felicity. "Stealing a locket from one of my closest friends and then ruining everyone's enjoyment. See you, with the good officers of the law, later!" She slammed the outer door on him, slipping another bolt into position.

As Felicity slid the final bolt, Robin's muffled voice came through the boards. "It's not just me, you know!"

"What?" called Chloe.

"I didn't do it on my own, so you're not as clever as you think."

"What does he mean?" asked Aiden.

"He's just being daft," said Felicity. "You caught him red handed. It has to be him."

"Who is he?" asked Chloe. "Where does he come from?"

"Oh − he's an art historian. He pokes around looking at old things in museums and art galleries. That'll be why he fancied that necklace. But I thought he was a friend. He's done so much research into the castle. So disappointing. Now, dears, let's get on with the play!"

CHAPTER 25

As darkness fell, excitement began to build. Diedre de Lhonghi was running everywhere with pins in her mouth, chopping and sculpting the costumes while the actors were trying to do their makeup.

Ava sat looking in the mirror. The makeup was weird thick stuff from the village hall that looked awful on her dark skin. She glanced around, all the other actors were putting dark lines under their eyes with pale eye shadows and red lips. She was still wondering quite what to do when Grandma stuck her head around the doorframe.

"Ava, love, just sorting out the refreshments, but brought you and Josh some makeup. Got Edward to go to town so he chose them, sorry, but I think these might do?" She held out a bag with assorted lipsticks and eyeshadows. The colours were vibrant, and when Ava tested the kingfisher blue eyeshadow on her arm, she knew she'd be just fine.

Beyond her, Josh was peering through the curtains. He was counting the number of people in the audience. "Ninety-six, and there are still a few empty chairs. Loads of people," he said. "There are absolutely loads."

"You nervous?" asked Jake, who was standing on the stage, reading his lines.

"What, me? Nah, never," said Josh, as if he was a seasoned performer. But in truth, Ava knew he was terrified. It had seemed such a good idea to take over Felicity's part, and he'd had a lot of fun, but now…

"I'm worried I won't remember my lines," said Jake.

"You'll be fine, we'll all be fine – anyway, Old Jeffers is going to sit in the wings with the prompt. Isn't he? And he's going to play Robin's part, I think?" Ava pointed to the prompt chair to the right of the stage. The only problem was that Jeffers was inclined to fall asleep.

"Hope you're right," said Jake. "I don't mind saying that this is well outside my comfort zone. Well outside."

And mine, thought Ava, swallowing.

The play began with the uncle and Aunt Maud on stage. The actors waited in the wings, the audience hushed. Chloe increased the volume of the curious creepy music that Felicity had chosen, and Aiden faded in the lights on the stage and faded out the lights over the audience.

Hush fell across the room and, as the music slipped away, Jeffers wound back the curtains.

CHAPTER 26

"Good morning, my love," said Jake, almost before the curtains had opened.

"Oh, my dove," replied Josh. "What a wonderful morning, what a wonderful day." He swept around in a circle, his cushions bumping into items of furniture, setting a small titter through the audience. Josh stopped and glared at them, sending a longer more audible laugh through the rows.

Ava watched, feeling so nervous she could barely open her mouth when it came to her turn. She stepped out on to the stage and swung to face the audience. For a second she was tongue tied, totally unable to remember a word. Behind her Josh whispered, "Good morning."

She took a deep breath and said, "Good morning," paused and then rattled out the rest of her lines, vaguely aware that Josh was waddling back and forth across the stage. She stopped and stared at him, he stopped and stared at her. The audience laughed. A door opened in the side of the hall and someone came in late, umbrellas fell to the ground, programmes were dropped, and Ava and Jake battled on.

From the gallery, Aiden watched Josh dying. When Felicity had been the murder victim, it was a quiet little croak. With Josh it was a full-on death rattle, followed by lots of staggering about and crashing into the furniture. The audience thought it was hilarious and, although he was kind of relaxed – after all, Robin Baird was behind bars – he was bothered by the last thing Baird had said: "It's not just me you know." Was that a wind up or was there really an accomplice?

He looked down at his script. Time for Old Jeffers to read Robin Baird's part, but to Aiden's amazement, a new figure appeared on stage. Stanislav? A murmur went through the audience and apart from Ava stalling and staring, the whole thing appeared to run smoothly.

The second half was very much more the play that Stanislav had originally directed. Serious. With long pauses and significant looks. On balance, Aiden thought the Josh pantomime version was more fun, but the audience were rapt. Half an hour in, four police officers slipped in through the back entrance and Grandma guided them to some empty seats.

At the end, the applause was massive. Encores and standing ovations and bunches of flowers were presented to Martha and a tearful Felicity, who made a short inaudible speech about community and determination which everyone seemed to love.

"Phew," said Chloe, bringing up the music. "What an evening!"

Aiden nodded. He couldn't even think of a reply.

"So, Stanislav, you knew all along? You beast – why

didn't you tell anyone?" croaked Felicity, when the audience had gone and the police were upstairs fingerprinting Robin Baird's room. Everyone was back in the rehearsal room wiping makeup from their faces and eyeing the mounds of bake-athon cakes, waiting for some rumoured hot chocolate.

"Dear Cecil showed it to me. I thought you knew, Martha. It was his most precious possession. But it never once occurred to me that Baird was so desperate to have it. I know he's an art historian, but I was under the impression he was above reproach."

"But how did he know it had a portrait inside?" asked Chloe.

Stanislav swept his scarf over his shoulder and let out a long sigh. "It might have been my fault. I did meet Baird once, and we talked about Hilliard miniatures. I might have told him that Cecil had one. He put two and two together."

"So, he wanted it for himself?"

"Oh, completely," said Stanislav. "They're the most exquisite things. Quite utterly precious. I'd love one. And Martha dear, you have one! You really are the luckiest girl."

Martha looked down at the locket around her neck. "I didn't know. I wouldn't have known if he hadn't tried to steal it. Would you have told me, Stanislav?"

"No – I was sure you knew. What an idiot I am."

"Not at all," said Martha. "Uncle Cecil was the idiot for not telling me." She smiled and gave Stanislav a hug. He flushed and hugged her back.

"It's you – isn't it?" said Aiden quietly.

"What?" said Stanislav. "What on earth do you mean?"

"You were the accomplice – you were the one that broke the car window in search of the box – and you were the one that hid the necklace in the courtyard. Robin Baird just came out to get it back. He ran through the passages, he searched Martha's bag in her room, he chased Ava and Josh. But you've been working together – until the end. Until he tried to grab it."

"Preposterous!" protested Stanislav. "Felicity, tell the boy who I am."

But Felicity narrowed her eyes and looked from Stanislav to Aiden to Martha. "You're a man who lost a lot of money on a series of dreadful plays," she said. "You're a man who has a hundred thousand reasons for wanting an original Hilliard. You're a man who knows the value of such a thing – and you're an actor."

"Does that make me guilty?" said Stanislav.

"It completely makes sense," said Chloe. "Doesn't it? And he had every opportunity – and he's tall enough."

Everyone stood in silence, staring at Stanislav. Slowly his shoulders sagged, and he sank to the sofa, hanging his head in his hands. He finally raised his head and looked at Martha.

"Oh, my dear, I'm so terribly sorry," he said, holding his hands out as if he was waiting to be cuffed. "I was desperate. I should never have listened to him."

"If you'll sit there quietly, and not race off around the castle, I'll call the police down from upstairs," said Felicity. "Unless, Aiden, love, you do it."

"So where's the real necklace?" asked Chloe.

"It's here," said Felicity, reaching into her pocket.

"May I?" asked Harry, holding the necklace out

and putting it around Martha's neck. "There − I don't know which is more beautiful, you or the famous queen inside."

Josh smothered a choking sound and just at that moment, Grandma Primrose, Grandpa Edward and Mrs Edge arrived with a tray of steaming chocolate and a pile of cheese on toast.

"Oh, wow," said Josh. "That looks amazing."

"Dig in, everyone," said Grandpa Edward. "Dig in, you deserve it. Not every day you rescue a queen's portrait!"

On their way back through the lanes, the cousins watched as snow began to fall again, blanketing the road and covering Grandpa's windscreen.

"Can we do nothing tomorrow?" asked Chloe, pulling Bella over her legs and yawning.

"We could have a snowball fight − a really big one," said Josh. "Imagine the yard, just right with those low walls."

"We could do both," said Aiden.

"We could do anything. Nothing. Everything," said Ava, sticking her hand out of the window and letting the snowflakes melt on her hand. "It's always so wonderful here – even doing nothing will give us a new adventure."

"We could always go sledging," said Grandma.

"And make scones," said Grandpa.

"So pleased I came," said Aiden. "That was just the best thing ever."

"Wasn't it just?" said Ava. "Can we do it all again next year?"

"Yeah – it was fabulosi," said Josh. "But right now, I'm still hungry – anything cooking, Grandpa?"

"Of course," said Grandpa, swinging the Land Rover into the entrance of Clifftopper Farm. "Isn't there always?"